DEDICATION

To JoAnn
Thanks for being there from the very start and
making this project possible

ALSO BY JESSICA SCOTT

The Coming Home Series

Because of You (ebook)
I'll Be Home for Christmas: A Coming Home
Novella (ebook)
Anything for You: A Coming Home Short Story
Back to You
Until There Was You (ebook)
All For You
It's Always Been You
All I Want for Christmas is You: A Coming Home
Novella

Nonficton

To Iraq & Back: On War and Writing
The Long Way Home: One Mom's Journey Home
from War

Chapter One

It was hell getting your heart ripped out right before Christmas.

And no matter how much scotch he threw at the problem, Major Patrick MacLean couldn't make the bleeding stop.

Sam was gone. And she'd taken Natalie with her.

Patrick knew all the stages of grief—at least a few of them. The anger. The denial. Maybe not in that order, but he knew how to deal with Seriously Bad Shit.

Except that he hadn't moved—not from the couch or from the bottom of the bottle that he'd crawled into at the start of the holiday half-day schedule.

On the coffee table in front of him, his cell phone vibrated violently.

He blinked rapidly a couple of times. The angry gadget was blurry and out of focus. He was on leave. He didn't have to answer the damn phone if he didn't want to.

At least, he didn't think he did. He *was* on leave, right? He'd signed out, right? He rubbed his temples, trying to think if he'd called the staff duty. Hell, he couldn't remember. He groped in the dark for the bottle as the phone went silent.

Except the damn thing started vibrating again.

Someone didn't know how to take a hint.

He snatched the phone off the table, too irritated to look at the number. "Yeah?"

"Daddy?"

He froze, the haze burning from his brain instantly. The wound Sam had left on his soul ripped open again at the sound of Natalie's voice. He closed his eyes, fighting to breathe against the tightness in his throat. Losing his family was worse, so much worse, than anything Iraq had thrown at him.

"Hey, sugar bear." He cradled his head in his hands, his heart breaking at the sound of her voice.

Natalie wasn't his daughter. Not by blood or legal paperwork.

But he was still her daddy. The only daddy she'd ever known, and in his heart, she was his.

She was his family. Sam was his family.

And they were gone. Just. Gone.

He cleared his throat.

"You're up late," he managed, hoping she didn't hear how bad he sounded to his own ears. "Shouldn't you be sleeping?"

"Something's wrong with Mommy."

Hello, Captain Obvious. He didn't say that, though. He wasn't sure the eight-year-old would appreciate the sarcasm. "Is she hurt?" he asked instead.

"She's crying all the time. And she doesn't talk to me." Her little voice broke. "I don't know how to make her okay."

"Are you okay?"

"No." A tiny, hitched breath. "I want to come home. I want to see you. Mommy… Something is wrong." A sniff, followed by a muffled sob. "Can you come get me?"

"Honey, you're all the way in Maine."

Silence for what felt like an eternity. "Isn't this why they have airplanes?"

He smiled at the deadpan voice. Nat had been working on her repertoire of smartass skills. Any other time, he would have been so proud. Except that his heart hurt at the sound of her voice.

"I—" His voice locked in his throat.

"Daddy, I'm scared." Another quiet sniff. "Please come. This was supposed to be our first Christmas together since you and Mommy came home from Iraq."

Damn. The kid was good at getting what she wanted. He'd told himself that she was too little to remember when he'd kissed her good-bye and gotten on that plane. That she wouldn't remember the phone calls when she'd cried that she wanted him to come home. That she *misted* him when she couldn't say *missed* right.

That maybe she was too little to notice that her mother had packed them off without so much as saying good-bye.

At some level, he'd rationalized that letting Sam go was the right thing to do. That if she wasn't happy anymore, it was better that she left before they started hating each other. That things had changed between them, and he should remember the good times.

It was obvious since she'd come home that something was wrong, but he hadn't pushed. He'd given her space, thinking she needed it to get things sorted in her head.

Except that space, apparently, had been the wrong thing to give.

"Please, Daddy."

He closed his eyes. And made a decision that was either going to damn him to hell or save the little girl and the family that he loved with all his heart.

***

It was still dark, the moonlight frozen on the path in front of her. The cold penetrated her bones and seeped into her soul. The only sound on the wooded path was the crunch of her boots on the frozen crust. The air froze in her nose and seared her throat, biting at her cheeks as she walked.

Captain Samantha Egan walked through the Maine woods where she'd grown up and felt like she didn't belong there anymore. She didn't belong anywhere. Not at Fort Hood. Not back home.

Everything felt wrong.

And she was cold. But it was more than cold from the temperature. No, it was the cold of something dead in the space where her heart had been. She was more used to the Iraqi heat—even in the dead of what passed for winter there—than the frigid central Maine subarctic temps.

She'd hoped that coming home to Saber Falls might jolt the dead space in her chest back to life. That the darkness would burn away in the bright sunlight sparkling off the frozen trees.

But it hadn't. She'd been home for a few days, back from the war in Iraq for less than a month, and nothing she did felt right. Not being around Natalie. Not being around her mother or her old friends from high school. Especially not being around friends from high school. She'd tried to stop in and see her friends Garrett and Finn Rierson but her lungs had stopped working before she'd even pulled into the police station where Garrett worked. She'd kept driving, avoiding the reality of seeing them. Avoiding the reality of the loss of her best friend that threatened to cut off her air every time she thought about her. She breathed out as she rounded a bend in the snowmobile trail, turning back toward her mother's house, trying to ease the automatic tightness in her chest when she thought about Mel.

The hole in her heart was matched by the hole left in their lives from the war.

Nothing felt right but work. Work and being around the soldiers she'd deployed with were the only things that didn't feel wrong.

Even then, being around the guys from work wasn't the same now that they were all home. She was the odd woman out as the men went home to their wives and the women went home to their husbands and kids.

She pulled her hat down over her ears, trying to keep out the penetrating cold.

Sam had gone home to her daughter. To the man who'd been a part of her life for the last nine years.

And she'd felt nothing.

No joy at seeing Natalie. No happiness at being with Patrick.

Oh, she'd smiled and said all the right things. But inside, something special was broken. There were no words for the utter lack of any feeling. Everything was mechanical and stilted. Off.

Especially with Patrick.

He was a good man. A man she'd loved with everything she was.

But things weren't the same anymore. Something had changed during her deployment. She'd stopped calling as much, unable to bear hearing her daughter's voice on the phone. The pain in her heart when her daughter cried for her ripped out her soul, made her question everything she was doing in the war, in the Army.

But it was different with Patrick. She'd stopped calling him, too; not just Natalie. She hadn't been able to deal with hearing about the homework or dinner or all the other normal things he did while she was deployed. He managed her being gone so much better than she'd done without him.

It wasn't like he hadn't deployed, too. She'd been the worried other half on the other side of the world before.

Maybe the war had taken her ability to feel any happiness at all ever again. The deployment …the deployment had broken her ability to feel anything for him, and she couldn't say why, only that now she looked at him and felt…nothing. She'd hoped, prayed, that seeing him would make her feel again, would breathe life back into the dead spot in her chest.

But that first night home, when he'd slid into the bed next to her, she'd feigned sleep and denied them both. She sucked in a deep breath, letting the cold burn in her lungs until her eyes watered.

He was no warrior saint. What she'd done—or rather what she hadn't done—had hurt them both. She'd seen his hurt and the anger and frustration just there beneath the surface.

But it hadn't cracked the frozen glass encasing her heart.

She couldn't say what had happened to the love she'd felt for him. But after a week of pretending, she'd broken the news.

"I'm going home for Christmas," she'd said as he'd stripped in the bathroom after PT.

He'd turned slowly, his dark brown eyes filled with expectation and a thousand questions. "Okay?" he'd said cautiously.

"I'm not coming back," she'd said, her voice as flat as the emotions in her chest.

The veins in his neck had bunched, standing out against his skin. "Back to me or back to the Army?"

She looked away from the penetrating concern in his eyes. Patrick was a good man. A strong man. A man who had loved her daughter and who had loved her.

And she wasn't capable of loving him back anymore.

It was better to end it now. Cauterize the wound before it festered and grew in hatred and anger. Maybe they could figure out how to be friends.

Maybe someday, when things weren't all wilted and frayed inside her.

"I'm sorry," was all she had managed.

Walking through the woods now, she couldn't say when things had gone wrong. She couldn't put a mark on the calendar that she could pinpoint and say *here's when things went to shit* in her life.

She'd hoped coming home would fix things. That the fog would clear away and she'd feel *something* again. But the fog was still there.

And it still felt like she was looking at life from very far away.

So she walked. Through the woods as the sun slid higher over the frozen Maine trees and hills, hoping that something would snap her out of it.

There was no reason for her to feel this way.

She'd made it home from the war when others hadn't. She had a daughter who was healthy and a man who'd taken care of their lives while she was deployed. A career that she was damn good at.

She'd come home.

She just didn't know what that actually felt like.

She didn't know if she'd ever feel again.

But she had to keep going. Had to put one foot in front of the other. She just needed to suck it up and snap herself out of it.

Because she had a daughter to raise. And the war was far from over.

For her, it would never be over. The ghosts would be with her, no matter how far she walked or how hard she tried to pretend they weren't.

Her toes burned from the cold. She needed to get warm. Maybe Mom and Natalie wouldn't be up yet so she could sit by the fire and just let the heat seep into her bones.

Natalie was an early bird, though. All those mornings of getting up for daycare since she was a baby had set the little bugger's internal clock for the ass-crack of dawn. Maybe, though, maybe today she'd sleep in.

It was Christmas, right? Miracles could happen.

Sam had promised her a trip to see Santa. Damn, but she didn't want to drive the hour to Bangor to the mall. She used to love coming home to Central Maine for a visit, but she damn sure hated the thirty-minute drive for the nearest real grocery store or the hour plus to Bangor.

But she'd promised and, well, a promise was a promise.

So if the weather held, she'd bundle her little bear up and head to the mall.

But first she needed to get warm. Badly.

She opened the sliders to her mother's back door. She'd always loved her mom's house. The back of the house faced away from the road and civilization in general. It was peaceful.

She kicked the snow off her boots and slid the door shut behind her.

There was movement in the kitchen. The light was on now. Probably Mom. Guess Natalie's early riser tendencies were genetic. "Mom?"

Silence greeted her question.

She frowned.

Then froze as the shadows near the kitchen sink moved and morphed into the man she'd abandoned.

Patrick stepped into the pale morning light.

"Hi, Sam."

Chapter Two

She wasn't sleeping.

Damn it, she looked good. Her cheeks were flushed, her lips red from the cold. Her dark hair stuck out from beneath the cap she'd worn. He almost smiled. It was her PT cap.

You could take the soldier out of Fort Hood and all that...

He didn't want to notice how seeing her made his guts tighten and his heart race. He focused on the tired lines around her mouth, rather than how seeing her made the anger and the hurt and the longing surface all at once. It was all churning together, twisting around inside him and making him wish for things that he couldn't have.

Her lips parted but no sound came out.

"Natalie called me," he said quietly.

"No one told me you were coming." Her voice was quiet and cold. Brittle.

Like she was one step away from the edge of a cliff.

"I didn't tell anyone." He stuffed his hands in his pockets because he couldn't think of what to do with them.

"You should have called."

"Would it have mattered?" He wasn't going to apologize for coming to Maine to see his daughter. Damn it, he wasn't going to let Sam take that away from him while she sorted out whatever the hell was going on with her.

She closed her eyes, and he could see the strain on her lips, in the tired lines of her neck. "Where are you staying?"

"At the bed and breakfast next to Finn's place." Finn Rierson had become a friend of Patrick's over the years.

"They're not booked this time of year?"

This polite conversation was strained, like something that happened between strangers.

"Guess not."

She said nothing, and just like that the conversation petered out. She stood there for a moment, still and cold.

She shivered and turned to strip off her coat. He watched her move, part of him so fucking grateful that she'd made it home from the war.

A man wasn't supposed to send his lover off while he stayed home with the kids. No matter how liberated he was, no matter how much he knew she loved her life in the Army, he'd worried about not being there to protect her. To keep her safe.

Guess he'd gotten familiar with how Army wives had felt. The year he'd had with Natalie when Sam had been gone had given him new respect for what she'd gone through when he'd deployed and a newfound respect for life on the home front. He'd counted down the days until she came home.

But the woman who stood before him now, shivering in the doorway, stripping off her coat and boots, wasn't the same woman he'd kissed good-bye all those months ago.

There had been distance on this deployment. Too much time between phone calls, short stuttered e-mails. No response to the notes he'd sent her telling her that he missed her. He'd been so busy with Natalie that he'd held out hope it was all his imagination. But when she'd come home, his fears had been manifested in reality.

The floor above his head creaked, followed by small, muffled footsteps. A moment later, a sleepy Natalie shuffled down the stairs. Patrick's heart melted as she rubbed her eyes. She hadn't seen him yet. She was tired and rumpled and adorable. Her hair was a twisted mess. She must have gone to sleep with her hair wet.

That had been a fun lesson to learn when he'd stepped into the role of primary parent. Sam had always taken care of putting Natalie to bed but when she'd gone, Patrick had gotten a crash course in little girl hygiene requirements. Put the kid to bed with wet hair, wake up with a rat's nest to comb through.

Which was always so much fun when trying to get out the door at five-thirty in the morning.

She stopped at the bottom step. Paused and blinked slowly.

Then her face lit up, and with a burst of energy, she shot across the small space, a happy cry of "Daddy!" filling the void in his heart.

He scooped her up, holding her close and breathing in the scent of her. She was clean and safe and warm.

She was his little girl.

"You came." She nestled close with a happy sound.

He caught Sam's eyes over Natalie's shoulder. Her expression was blank, but in her eyes was a hint, the barest hint of something beyond the dead, listless stare he'd seen since she'd come home from Iraq.

He wanted to shake her, to push her to snap out of it. To bring back the woman he'd fallen for all those years ago when she'd let him into her home and her life. A life that had included a baby girl that he'd fallen hopelessly in love with the moment she'd entered the world.

He didn't know how to fix things. He didn't know how to fix her.

And because of that, he was losing everything that mattered in this life.

Natalie leaned back. "Will you come with us to see Santa today?"

His gaze collided with Sam's. He saw her open her mouth. Braced for the denial. Braced for her to ask him to leave.

To ask him to stop being a father to the little girl in his arms.

"Honey, I'm sure Daddy's tired. It's a long flight from Texas to Maine."

Patrick stilled, analyzing her response. Her words bounced around his brain, seeking some point of reference before he recognized that she hadn't said no.

"What time are you going?" he asked when he could find his voice without risking embarrassing himself.

That feeling, that choking, uncertain feeling was hope modulated by pure terror.

"I was thinking about noon," she said quietly. "You could get settled first. Maybe take a nap if you wanted."

He tried to keep the surprise off his face and was pretty sure he failed.

Natalie bounced down and rushed to her mother. "Thank you! This way Grammy can go visit Mr. Thomas and have Grammy and Thomas time."

Patrick choked. He didn't want to know if "Grammy and Thomas time" meant what he thought it meant. He'd known Nancy and Thomas were close since the first time he'd come home with Sam. Natalie raced back up the stairs, yelling for Grammy. If Nancy had been trying to go back to sleep, she definitely wasn't now.

He'd always liked Samantha's mother. Nancy Egan hadn't approved of her daughter's choices, but she'd never breathed a rude word toward Patrick. When he'd shown up on her doorstep that morning, the only thing she'd done other than let him in the house was make coffee and then go back to bed.

Patrick watched Sam closely at the mention of her best friend's father. Had she seen Thomas since she'd been home? Sam may have lost her best friend but Thomas had lost a daughter.

How on earth was Sam coping with her death? He looked at her then, seeing the too-familiar grief looking back at him. He wanted to ask, to say something that would make the pain easier to bear.

But nothing, not even time would do that. It would sneak up on her, again and again over the years.

It was something no one told you about going to war. That it never really leaves you when you come home.

"I'm sorry, Sammy," he whispered.

She turned away, but not before he saw the tears glittering in her eyes, and his heart broke for her all over again.

***

Her lungs hurt. It felt like a massive sucking chest wound that ripped open all at once with the mention of Mel.

She thought she'd made her peace with her best friend's death on that convoy.

But standing there in her mother's kitchen beneath the sparkling white Christmas lights, her chest felt tight, her lungs compressed.

She couldn't breathe.

All she could do was feel.

And it fucking hurt.

She swiped at her cheeks, blinking and trying desperately to shove the emotion back down where she could pretend it wasn't a live thing, choking off her air.

That her heart wasn't shattering into a thousand pieces in her chest.

She felt rather than heard him move. One minute, she was standing alone at her mother's sliding glass doors, her reflection staring back at her through the frozen glass.

The next, a shadow stood behind her.

His hands were strong on her shoulders, the heat from his palms radiating through the chill in her bones.

He was solid and steady behind her. A thousand emotions surged inside her, storming toward the gates, threatening to drop her to her knees.

It was too much. The sympathy in his touch, the ragged pain in her chest, the burning behind her eyes.

She sucked in hard, deep breaths, wrestling everything back into the box that she locked then threw into the darkest corner of the abyss where she could safely ignore it.

She'd deal with the emotions in that box some other day.

It was only when she was certain she wouldn't shatter that she turned to face him.

And felt the loss immediately as his hands slipped from her shoulders.

"Natalie is glad you're here," she finally said carefully as tiny feet pounded on the ceiling above them.

A neutral topic. One she could handle.

She hoped.

"She was pretty upset when she called me," he said. He didn't move, but he didn't crowd her either. He was simply there. Right there. All she had to do was reach for him. A single touch to cross the chasm between them.

It wouldn't fix things, wouldn't fix them. Because it wasn't their relationship that needed to be fixed. It was her. And she had no idea how to say the three hardest words in the English language. *I need help.*

"What did she say?" Sam asked, steering her thoughts away from the emptiness inside her.

His eyes reflected the frozen landscape in the glass behind her. Dark and whip-smart and so often filled with laughter.

Today they were filled with worry.

"That something was wrong." His voice was thick, filled with recrimination.

"She's not wrong." It hurt to admit that.

"I can't help if you don't tell me what's wrong, Sam."

She retreated a single step, her back colliding with the slider behind her. The cold seeped through her fleece. "You can't fix this, Patrick." *You can't fix me.*

"So that's it? You're just going to walk away and take my daughter and leave, and I don't even get an explanation as to why?"

"She's not—"

"Don't." He held up one hand, shutting down the words she'd been about to speak. His eyes flashed violently. "Don't tell me she's not mine. We never got around to the paperwork, but I've raised that little girl like she was my own. Don't you dare say she's not mine."

Sam swallowed the lump in her throat. "Patrick."

He shook his head and stepped away, out of her space. "I can't do this right now. Do you want to meet here or at the place I'm staying for the trip to go see Santa?"

"You don't have to go. You look exhausted."

He pinned her with a deadpan look. "That's what happens when you catch a red-eye to the middle of nowhere because your daughter says she's scared."

She wasn't prepared to deal with his anger. She supposed that was why she'd told him and then left the following day.

She hadn't wanted a confrontation. She'd been hoping things could just... dissolve quietly. Without any nastiness.

He hadn't fought her when she'd said she was leaving. She'd assumed that meant he was relieved. That he was going to just let her go.

But he was here now.

"You didn't have to come. You could have just called me."

"Phone calls didn't seem to be the right way to discuss things," he said quietly.

Hell, she'd run away to Maine in order to put some distance between them. Because obviously the distance between them for the last year hadn't been enough.

She could see his reflection in the glass behind her. The worry in his eyes. The hurt.

It was her fault. He was a good man. He didn't deserve this.

And yet she couldn't find any feelings in her heart for him. There was simply nothing there. She hadn't wanted to hurt him. She hadn't meant to. She'd only wanted to stop hurting him, to stop feeling like nothing mattered. To stop feeling afraid that if she said those three little words, he would turn away from her in disgust at her weakness that she hadn't been able to go to war after all. That she would lose her lover because she'd lost her ability to feel and she was ashamed to admit it.

She'd thought she'd been hiding what was wrong with her. One look at Patrick told her otherwise.

And she'd lost him anyway because she could no longer remember what loving him felt like.

But she couldn't be around him and remember that once upon a time, she'd felt something for him. Standing there now, facing him, was just a reminder of something else she'd lost along the way home from war.

And she hated it. Hated the war. Hated the pointlessness of it.

So why did she stay in the Army? Wasn't that the hundred–thousand-dollar question?

"I don't want to do this right now, Patrick." Words filled with sadness and regret. "We can talk about how to split things up after Christmas."

The patient, steadfast Patrick she'd fallen in love with all those years ago was there but he was angry now. And hurt. He stepped into her space.

His hands were rough where they slid over her cheeks. He didn't stop his advance until she was pressed between the cold glass behind her and the raw heat of the man in front of her.

"You act like things are already over," he said fiercely. "They're not."

And then he kissed her.

***

He didn't know what pushed him to invade her space. He couldn't say what happened between the moment the idea formed in his head and moving. But part of him needed to feel, to touch her and remind himself that she was real, not simply a shadow of the woman who had left him.

He had to know.

But then her skin was cool and soft beneath his palms. Her body was hard and warm against his, her lips soft and warm and *Sam*.

They parted with a gasp. It was a shock to them both as he took, demanding access to her secrets and her pain and everything she was holding back from him.

From them.

Because this distance—this wasn't just about physical distance.

She was his best friend.

And he kissed her like he was dying without her.

Because he was.

He wanted his Samantha back. The warrior goddess who'd laughed when they'd been at the range and she'd outshot him. The fierce lover who took her own pleasure while driving him wild.

The woman who didn't take shit from anyone.

He kissed her like it was his first taste of pleasure in months.

Because it was.

Her response was a deep, shuddering thing between them. One hand curled around his forearm as he claimed them both, held nothing back. Poured everything he was into that kiss and told her without words that he wasn't giving up on her without a fight.

The briefest flare of passion and then it was over.

But it wasn't. She was still in there. His Sam was there. Damaged and afraid, but there. He'd felt her in that kiss, the echo of the love they'd felt for each other.

He stepped back, knowing he was leaving her off-kilter and unbalanced and knowing there was nothing else he could do.

"I'll meet you here in an hour."

And he was gone before she could protest.

Because in that kiss, Patrick had made a decision.

That kiss wasn't a kiss that said they were over. She'd responded to his touch, she'd swayed against him. He knew in his bones that had they been alone, he might have been able to press his advantage and find a way into the dark where she was trapped.

If there ever was a time for a Christmas miracle, now would be the time, he thought as he drove out of the snow-packed drive and turned onto Route 16, heading into the tiny little town of Saber Falls.

He didn't have a plan. He didn't have a fairy godmother to tell him what was wrong so he could figure out how to fix it.

But if the war had taught him anything, it was that time was so very precious.

He was going to figure this out.

Because if he lost her and Natalie, he'd have truly lost everything.

Chapter Three

Why hy are you being so quiet, peanut?"

Patrick glanced in the rearview mirror at Natalie. Her little brown head was bowed, and she was scribbling on a piece of paper.

There was no kicking the seat, no whining about having to pee five minutes after leaving the gas station.

There was just silence.

And silence plus kids always equaled trouble.

He'd learned that the hard way when Sam had first deployed, too. He'd thought he'd have a nice Sunday afternoon watching football while Natalie played in her room. He'd dozed off, only to wake up in a panic when he realized he hadn't heard a peep from her in who knew how long.

She'd been painting the bathroom floor. With nail polish. Which had been much harder to get off porcelain tile than he'd been prepared for. He'd also learned the difference that day between acetone and non-acetone nail polish remover. And hadn't that been a fun conversation to have in the middle of Wal-Mart with a little old lady who looked ready to call

Child Protective Services because Natalie was out in public in pajamas, a bath robe, and bunny slippers. At three in the afternoon.

He smiled at the memory.

"Nat?"

She looked up. "Nothing, Daddy. Just writing a letter to Santa."

He glanced over at Sam, who shrugged and remained quiet.

"What are you going to ask him for?"

She looked up at him, and he saw her mother looking back at him from those somber blue eyes. "I can't tell you that. It's a secret."

"Baby, it's a secret when you blow out your birthday candles and make a wish. It's not a secret to tell us what you're going to ask Santa for."

She shook her head. "Nope. Not telling."

He saw Sam's lips curl in a faint smile before turning his attention back to the logging truck in front of him.

That kiss stood between them like a live thing, demanding attention and unwilling to be ignored.

And yet, Sam was doing her best to pretend nothing had happened. That he hadn't seen the spark in her eyes when he'd stepped away. That she wasn't gone.

But she was still there. Hiding. Deep in the shadows.

All he had to do was figure out a way to draw her out, back into the light.

He sighed quietly and focused on the road. A better man might have let her go. Might have cut his losses with a woman who was, even after nine years together, still skittish. Still didn't trust that he wouldn't cut and run.

That he was not her father or the man who'd left her high and dry.

"How was your flight up?" he asked, trying to fill the silence.

"Fine."

"Well, let's not waste too much air on conversation, now shall we?"

She shot him a bland look. "I'd rather not do this with little ears in the car, if it's all the same to you."

A tiny voice chirped up from the back seat. "Are you two getting divorced?"

Patrick glanced over at Sam, who looked just this side of horrified.

"No, honey, we're not getting divorced," Sam said quietly. "Why do you know what divorce even is?"

"My friend Elsa's parents are getting divorced. She said her mommy called her daddy a two-timing pig. What's a two-timing pig?"

Patrick rubbed his hand over his mouth to keep from smiling. Sam was less than impressed.

"It means that her parents aren't going to live together anymore," Sam said gently.

Patrick glanced at Natalie. She tapped the pencil against her cheek. "So if you and me move to Maine and Daddy stays in Texas, how is that not divorce?"

Patrick felt slightly ill. He sighed quietly. "It means Elsa's parents aren't going to be married anymore. Your mommy and I aren't married, so we can't get divorced."

And holy hell, he did not want to do this right now. Talk about making it difficult to pay attention to the truck in front of him.

"Why aren't you married?"

"It's a long story, honey," Sam said. "It hasn't mattered before."

Except that it damn sure mattered now. Patrick tried not to be bitter.

Patrick cleared his throat. "Why don't you work on your letter to Santa some more?" he said, hoping, praying that she would drop it and knowing that she probably wouldn't. She was usually incessant with questions.

So the silence that came out of the back seat ended up being quite a surprise. After a while he looked back in the rearview to see she was still busy writing.

"What the heck could an eight-year-old be writing that takes so long?" he asked Sam beneath his breath.

"She's always had an active imagination."

There was nothing more to say, because Sam was right. The things that needed to be said couldn't be said in front of Natalie.

Instead, there was only silence as the drive continued.

***

Sam took a deep breath as they stepped out of the cold and into the cavernous mall entrance.

It hadn't changed much since she'd worked there as a teen. She'd been so excited when she'd gotten a job at Chess King. It had been so cool to have a job in the mall.

The Chess King was gone now, replaced by some place that sold purses and Maine kitsch. She wasn't sure who at the mall would buy the refrigerator magnets or bumper stickers. Probably for folks who lived out of state now or had friends who visited.

She'd braced for the overwhelming sense of the familiar.

She did not count on the anxiety that slithered around her chest, squeezing like a wet wool blanket.

She looked back for Natalie. "Nat, honey, hold my hand."

Patrick looked over at her, a question in his eyes.

"I don't want her to wander off," Sam said.

The fear was relentless, a pressure on the back of her neck that made her want to keep turning around. She rubbed Natalie's hand, trying to focus on anything other than the sensation of being unable to breathe.

Patrick's hand on her shoulder startled her. Her breath lodged in her throat.

"Sam." His voice was gentle, his touch strong. "We can go," he said quietly. "We don't have to do this right now."

She blinked rapidly. There was no judgment in his voice, no condemnation.

Simply understanding.

She smiled sadly. "We just drove an hour."

"Are you okay?"

"I have to be, don't I?"

He slipped his hand over her neck, cradling her. "Not all the time. No."

She bit her bottom lip and looked away. Wishing she could explain the pressing fear on her heart. Wishing she could make the insurgent trepidation go away and leave her alone.

Wishing she could have a normal day at the mall with her daughter to go see Santa. But she couldn't. Because she had decided that going to war was going to be a day at the damned beach. She hadn't counted on the fear of getting blown up in a convoy grafting itself violently onto the fear of losing her daughter in a mall. They were not even remotely related and yet she knew that one had led to the other. There was simply no other source.

She'd done this before—gone to the mall and gone shopping like a normal person. Before the deployment. Before she'd spent days on the roads with her battalion commander.

She'd been fine before the war.

Now? Now she was just this side of a paranoid basket case. And wasn't that a fun way to spend the day?

She was *not* going to ruin her daughter's trip to see Santa.

She sucked in a deep breath. "Thank you for saying that, Patrick," she said softly.

She met his gaze then. Saw the worry and the concern.

But it was the hurt that struck at her. The hurt that lashed out and resurrected the guilt she'd been trying to ignore. Because leaving him had not been an easy choice.

It had simply felt like the only choice. Cut him free from the dead weight. Let him be with someone else. Someone not broken by the war. Someone who could admit there was something broken and get help and get better. Not her, who was terrified of those three little words.

A full-blown person rather than a shadow.

Maybe someday, she'd finally feel normal again. Maybe then, she could start unpacking everything that had happened. But for right now, she needed to lock things down. Needed to keep the box sealed tight.

Because the darkness within was just itching to get out.

And she was not prepared to deal with that emotional tidal wave.

Better to walk away. To leave sleeping things where they lay.

"Mommy, let's gooo."

She let herself be tugged away. Felt his hand slip from her neck and the cool kiss of air where the heat from his touch had been.

He stayed with her, though. He walked by her side, keeping an eye on her, she knew.

He was good like that.

The war hadn't broken him like it had broken her. She wondered why. What was it about her that hadn't been able to handle the boring days, the long hours, the relentless stress? He'd lost friends. Good friends. He'd deployed three times to her one tour.

Why was he okay and she wasn't?

They found their place in line. Sam tried not to scan the crowds. Tried to enjoy listening to Natalie chatter on about Santa and Rudolph and the elves.

Instead, all she could focus on was Patrick standing behind her. Warm and solid and silent. Not trying to argue with her. Not shaming her or demanding what the hell was wrong with her that she couldn't relax.

It should be easy, to turn to him. To say *something is wrong. I want to get help. But I'm afraid.* But it wasn't easy. Even with him there, solid and steady behind her. Guarding her back.

Just like always.

Chapter Four

Who knew seeing Santa was that exhausting?" Sam murmured. "She's out cold."

Patrick glanced in the rearview, confirming Sam's assessment that Natalie was indeed asleep in the back seat, laid out across the bench seat, the seatbelt tucked around her chest and hips. He glanced over at Sam, trying to gauge how she was coping with everything. He'd seen her skittishness at the mall, remembered it well. The panicked feeling of too many people, of no easy access to cover. It wasn't a rational fear but that didn't mean it wasn't real.

It had taken him a long time to put those instinctive reactions behind him and even then, they were still there, a latent energy that sometimes snuck up on him.

"She's not the only one who needs a nap," Patrick said quietly.

"You didn't sleep when you left earlier?"

"No. Dropped off my stuff, got some coffee, and met you at the house." He was more relaxed than he'd been earlier. Less tense once they'd left the mall.

He'd watched her trying so hard to be normal. Trying so hard to pretend that she was just another parent at the holidays, trying to squeeze in a visit with Santa in the chaos of last minute shopping.

But she wasn't a normal parent. She was a mother who'd deployed to Iraq.

It had dawned on him when they'd first stepped into the mall and he'd seen the fear etched into the lines around her mouth, the panic in her eyes.

This was more than having a hard time adjusting to being home. There was a very real thing going on with her, and he figured out in that moment that she was trying to ignore all of it.

She was trying to do what so many soldiers did: stuff down the uncomfortable and unsettling thoughts and emotions. Lock them away and pretend that nothing about the war was out of the ordinary.

Pretend that deployment was just another day at the office, except that the office was now half a world away. Ignore the fact that sometimes, you needed help in coming home.

When you were deployed, there were no trips home to reset the mind. To release the tension and the stress until the next day.

No, whether you were out walking the streets or working at a desk, the stress was constant. The fear of a mortar didn't only haunt the infantrymen or the maneuver forces. Patrick knew that all too well.

And until she dealt with everything that'd happened to her downrange, she would never come home. Not fully. He wondered if she'd even considered seeing Doc back at the unit. Doc could point her in the right direction. Keep things quiet for her.

"There's a Dunkin' Donuts off Broadway on the way home," she suggested.

"That is a brilliant idea."

They drove in silence for a little bit before they stopped to order coffee, being careful not to wake Natalie. She'd normally sleep through a train wreck, but that didn't mean he wanted to test that theory.

There was so much he couldn't say with Natalie in the car. But there were other things he could.

"When I came home from that first tour, I hated leaving the house." He kept his voice neutral, his words soft. Not some big revelation of a tragic homecoming. Just a statement of what had been. "I couldn't stand going to the grocery store and listening to people complain about the lines or about Wal-Mart being out of their favorite toilet paper."

She cracked the barest smile. "I was so happy when we got to the FOB that we had a real toilet. And showers. We were always out of toilet paper, though. I carried a roll in one of my cargo pockets."

"I can see where that would be a problem." This was such a simple conversation. Like they were talking about the weather instead of latrine conditions in a war zone. "You know, if I ever deploy again, I'm going to take pictures of all the Porta-Potty graffiti. Maybe write a book about it."

"Valuable history, huh?" she said dryly.

"Some of it was pretty good. 'Course, I can't imagine hanging out in a Porta-Potty long enough to draw some of it."

She snorted softly. "That's some dedication right there."

"Well, there wasn't much else to do."

"You have a very limited imagination if drawing on latrine walls is all you can think of to pass the time in Iraq." Her voice thickened a little at the mention. Just a hint of emotion but enough that he noticed it, now that he was looking for it.

"Well, I didn't exactly have free time. I worked pretty much round the clock. Except Sundays. Sundays were the big sleep days."

"We did that too. There was always a movie playing at the chow hall after evening chow."

Silence stretched between them. He wanted to ask her what she was thinking about. Were there other memories that haunted her beyond losing Melanie?

"It's funny the things I remember. Like I remember how the gravel felt beneath my boots and the mural on the T-wall outside the chow hall. But all the days? Most of them blended together." His throat tightened as memories circled, just out of reach. Sensations, really.

"Except for the ones that stand out." She looked out into the cold Maine afternoon.

He reached for her then, daring to cross the chasm between them and rest his hand on her shoulder. A tentative gesture. One meant to offer comfort. Solace.

Understanding.

His breath lodged in his throat when she covered his hand with hers.

"Yeah, there were a few of those." He twined his fingers with hers. "More than a few I wish I could forget."

She didn't look at him, keeping her focus at the hazy winter sky. "I haven't slept well. Not since about halfway through my tour."

A quiet admission. He could guess how much it cost her to admit but it was an opening too precious to ignore.

"Did you ask Doc for some Ambien? Maybe talk to someone about not sleeping?"

"No." That single word was laced with fear. She unthreaded their fingers, slipping away from him once more with that quiet admission.

He swallowed, tapping his thumb on the lid of his coffee mug before taking a sip, buying himself some time. He wanted to push her, to ask her why she was trying so hard to be so tough when she clearly needed to talk to someone. Hell, it didn't have to be him, but someone. Anyone.

Instead, he took a deep breath and chose a different tactic. "My first tour, I worked eighteen-hour days. Nonstop. I remember curling up under my desk to catch a nap, then I'd get back up and keep going." A deep breath. "I hit the wall about eight months in. Punched my ops sergeant major for taking my last RipIt."

She looked at him, a single eyebrow arched. "You punched someone over a RipIt?"

"And some copier toner. It was already a tense relationship. Then he used the last of the toner for no smoking signs around the TOC when I had a packet to prepare for the brigade commander. I missed my briefing and got my ass handed to me. Then he took my last RipIt, and it was all over." He smiled flatly. "I don't actually remember doing it. My boss at the time was less than impressed that his brand new captain socked his senior NCO. Sent me to the doc, and ordered me to get some sleep." He shrugged. "So I kind of appreciate what a good night's sleep can do for the soul."

A long moment stretched between them. "I don't even remember what that feels like."

He hesitated, unsure how far he could push this relative truce.

"Maybe when we get back to Texas, talk to Doc. Can't hurt, right?"

***

Can't hurt, right? She let his words sink in, turned them over in her mind. He wanted her to talk to Doc. For sleep meds. She'd thought about it, so many times. Had even gone so far as to make an appointment with Doc only to cancel it at the last minute. Because fear was such a powerful thing.

Can't hurt, right?

Except that yeah, it could hurt. A lot. Because what if it didn't work? What if she was well and truly broken and nothing would ever help put her back together again?

She sighed softly. "I tried an Ambien once. Terrible nightmares and woke up feeling like hell the next day." She badly needed to turn the subject into something safer. Something that involved less soul-baring intensity.

She wasn't ready to unpack everything that happened in Iraq. Yet somehow, they'd just carried on a completely normal conversation without dredging up bad memories or worse.

And he wanted her to talk to Doc.

It was a completely normal conversation between two people pretending to be normal about a situation that was everything but normal.

He took a sip of his coffee. "I had a sergeant major who chewed them like they were Tic Tacs. Said it took five of them to knock him out every night."

She looked over at him. "The RipIt sergeant major?"

"Nah, this was my second tour. He'd stayed in and volunteered to do back-to-back tours to put his kid through Johns Hopkins Medical School."

"Why do I feel like you're not making that up?"

He covered his heart with one hand. "Swear to God. Sarn't Major Megholtz. Meanest SOB you ever met. Daughters had him wrapped around their little fingers."

"Sounds like someone else I know," she said quietly.

He glanced back at Natalie. "She's a good kid." His words were suddenly thick.

Her heart ached at the love in that simple sentence. "You're a good dad."

He said nothing for a long moment. The muscles in his neck bunched, his knuckles tensed on the steering wheel. "Whatever happens between us, Sam, please don't take my daughter." His voice cracked a little in the fading afternoon light.

She closed her eyes at the pain in those words. Pain she'd caused. She folded her arms over her chest and sank into the seat, struggling to hold in the wave of sadness his words sent surging.

There was nothing she could say to make things right. Nothing to take back the hurt she'd inflicted on him.

Nothing to make her feel the happiness that she should feel when he was around her daughter. The joy and the gladness that her daughter would grow up with a father who would be there for her. Who wouldn't leave her.

But Patrick was a soldier. And soldiers who went to war sometimes didn't come home. She knew that now. Up close and personal. And the thought of him at war again while she waited at home...

The sadness was back. Seeping out of the box. Threatening to destroy the latches and the hinges and send everything crashing over her.

She couldn't do it. It was easier not to feel. Easier to pretend she didn't care. Easier to pretend she didn't need help, that she'd snap out of it if she just tried harder to feel normal.

If she told herself she didn't care often enough, maybe it would be true. Because not caring was the only way to survive his next deployment.

Or hers.

God, how was she going to get on that plane again and leave Natalie? What if she didn't come home?

What if she was like Mel? There one day, gone the next.

Who would Natalie have left? Her biological father? That scumbag had no claim on Natalie. His name wasn't on her birth certificate. He could never come back and hurt her if anything ever happened to Sam.

Patrick was the only father she'd ever known. And he was a good father. A good man.

She trusted him with Natalie.

She just didn't trust herself with him anymore.

"Where'd you go just then, Sam?" he asked quietly.

"Nowhere." She sniffed. "You can't fix this."

"Maybe not." A cautious pause. "But we won't know unless we try. We haven't even tried. You…you just left."

She couldn't answer for the longest time. Her throat closed off and her eyes burned. She swiped at her cheeks, trying to keep the tears at bay.

Her voice broke when she finally managed the words. "I don't want to take Natalie from you."

"This isn't just about Natalie, Sam. This is about you. This is about us."

They rolled to a stop at a random light in the middle of nowhere. He turned to face her. "This isn't over yet. And the sooner you accept that, the better off all of us will be."

"Maybe it's been over a long time…we've just both been gone too much to see it."

"And maybe we've just been gone too much to remember how to be us," he snapped. There was steel in those words. Resolve that she was so intimately familiar with. "We haven't had that. There's been no you and me. We've both been working our asses off since the war started. We don't know how long this damn thing is going to go on. We don't know when it's going to end, when we'll finally get to be a normal family again. But we damn sure won't get that chance if we just cut sling load because the first time we're together again after almost two years, things don't fall magically back into place."

She shifted in her seat, his words hitting her at center mass, dead in the heart.

"I wish I had a better answer for you." Shame and fear laced those words. "But I don't. I'm sorry. But that's the best I've got to give."

He shook his head, the muscle in his jaw tensing. He looked at her then, his eyes furious and dark. "That's not good enough, Sam. Our family deserves better."

***

Patrick stopped at the gas station in Saber Falls, needing to fill up the rental car and a badly needed jolt of a ridiculously good cup of coffee to warm his blood. He'd come home with Sam in the past and the best cup of coffee north of Bangor was clearly the Green Mountain Coffee served there.

He always forgot to order some to take with him.

Maybe he'd remember this time, especially if this was going to be his last time here.

He sighed heavily, needing to clear space in his lungs for…oh, oxygen. Breathing was fundamental, but he couldn't do that with this elephant of sadness sitting on his chest.

He was not going to spend this entire trip sulking like a kicked puppy.

He knew Sam. He could figure this out, right? They'd been through rougher things before.

"Hey, Patrick, how's it going?"

He turned from the coffee to see Finn Rierson step into the gas station, followed by his cousin Garrett, the local sheriff. Sam always made it a point to see the Rierson boys every time they came home. The first time, Patrick had been mildly jealous, curious about these men that Sam had insisted on meeting at the Whistling River Pub.

But then he'd met them, and they were both damn hard to be jealous of.

They were good dudes. Friends from high school that Sam had refused to let go of even as life and the war and the Army kept her away from home for longer and longer periods.

And over time, they'd become his friends, too, so that he no longer felt like an awkward third wheel but part of the memories they shared every time they got together.

"I didn't know you were coming home," Garrett said. As though Saber Falls was as much his home as Sam's.

He supposed it was.

"It was an unexpected trip. Sam...really needed to come home after the year she's had."

"Yeah. The whole town was devastated when we lost Mel." Finn's voice was edgy and raw, the grief still sharp. A shadow crossed Finn's face and Patrick knew he was looking at a sadness that would never leave the other man. Mel and Finn...they'd been a thing, despite the war, despite the distance. And now she was gone, like so many others.

Finn took a step toward the coffee. Patrick only knew the fear of waiting for a lover to return from war, not the loss.

"I can't imagine what he's gone through," Garrett said quietly. "It was bad enough when I had to bury my parents and Derrick didn't come home."

Patrick frowned. "When did your folks die?"

"Last year. Right after Fourth of July."

"Ah hell, man, I'm really sorry." He'd only met Garrett's parents in passing but Joan and Ken Rierson had struck him as good people. "Derrick didn't come home?"

He'd never met Garrett's brother but had heard enough stories to know the prodigal son was missed.

"Said he couldn't get leave out of Iraq. Something about his unit not letting him go. That doesn't sound right."

"It happens. It all depends on the commander and what's going on at the time and how many people are already gone."

Finn sipped his coffee as he rejoined them. "I've got to get going. I've got a meeting over in Dover," Finn said. "It's good to see you, Patrick."

Patrick cleared his throat roughly. "You, too." He waited until Finn stepped out of the gas station and into the cold, the door shutting with a jingle behind him. "How's he holding up?"

"As good as he can, I guess. He stays busy." Garrett shrugged, and that was the end of the conversation. "Anyway, you and Sam should come out to the house. I've got some ice cleared off. You guys can skate on the pond."

"I'll ask her." He dumped cream—real cream—into his coffee. "She's been having a rough time of things since she's been home."

Garrett twisted the lid off his stainless steel thermos and reached for the darkest blend. "That doesn't sound like Sam. She's always so damn...fierce."

"Tell me about it." It felt strange to talk about this. He hadn't told anyone at work about things going to shit after Sam had gotten home. The couple

47

of guys he'd been close to had their own *stuff* going on.

He'd just tried to muscle through. Until Sam had left him.

He looked up from his coffee to find Garrett watching him. "Something you want to talk about?"

Patrick tested his coffee, buying time. "Sam left me."

Garrett said nothing for a moment, focusing on twisting the lid back on his thermos. "So is this the last Christmas home or is this the surprise 'I'm here to fight for my woman' visit."

Patrick laughed bitterly. "You have been watching too many Lifetime movies, my friend."

Garrett grinned. "I have to go check on Mrs. Poole once a week. We sit for an hour, and I have to watch whatever's on while she tells me the entire plot, backstory, and spoilers."

"Dude, are you like even a real person? You sit with old ladies? Next thing you'll tell me you brake for squirrels or something."

"So? What's wrong with that?"

Patrick smiled. "Nothing. Nothing at all. And to answer your question, this is the 'I'm not letting her go without a fight' visit."

"She didn't know you were coming, did she?"

"Nope."

"And?"

"And we made it about six minutes before she tried to tell me that Natalie wasn't mine, and that we were over." They paid for their coffee and stepped out into the bitter cold morning. "Dear god, how do you people live in this kind of cold?"

"Where are you from originally?"

"Florida."

"Meh, you'd get used to it if you were here long enough."

Patrick shrugged. It wasn't like he was going to get a chance to get used to it. Not if Sam had her way and they were really over.

"She's not, you know," Garrett said after a moment. "Legally, Natalie isn't yours."

Patrick looked over at Garrett. "I've known you for a long time, and that is the single most fucked up thing I've ever heard you say."

"I'm a cop, Patrick. I deal with this shit all the time. It doesn't matter that you were there from the beginning. It doesn't matter that Nat calls you Daddy. Legally, you don't have a leg to stand on."

"I've got powers of attorney naming me her guardian when Sam deployed." But he felt his certainty slip away. He knew the law. Hell, he was a damn lawyer.

But *Only a foolish lawyer has himself as a client* wasn't a cliché for nothing.

"Damn it, Sam," he muttered.

Garrett gripped his shoulder. "You're going to try to fight a custody case for a little girl that has neither your name nor your blood in a region of the country that notoriously does not consider taking children away from their mothers for even the worst transgressions."

Patrick's mouth fell open. "I don't want to take her away from Sam. I just want to be part of her life. Sam's a good mom. She's just…"

"What?"

Patrick paused. "I wish I knew. It's like only part of her came home from the war." He sipped his coffee. The shock of heat burned against his partially frozen lips. "She's there, but she's not. It's like she's a shadow."

Garrett scoffed quietly. "I wish I didn't get that. The one time I've seen Derrick since the war started, he was definitely not in the moment."

"How is he?"

"I don't know. He's gone into complete radio silence since last year. I kind of went off on him for not coming home for the funeral, and well, we haven't talked since."

"I'm sorry."

Garrett shrugged. "I can't live my brother's life for him."

There was more there, but now wasn't the time or the place.

Patrick sighed after a long moment. "The war's fucked up everyone's life, hasn't it?"

Garrett snorted quietly. "Wars tend to do that, don't they?"

Patrick said nothing for a long moment. "Yeah, I guess they do."

Chapter Five

Sam wasn't sure how long she'd sat, alone in the sunroom, sorting through the myriad emotions riding roughshod through the landscape of her soul, listening to Natalie and her mom make cookies.

It was morning. She should have been finishing up last minute Christmas shopping but she couldn't summon the energy.

The wind slapped against the plastic her mom had used to insulate the sunroom. Sam curled up in the chair, cradling her mug of coffee, savoring the warmth.

Wishing the taste on her lips was still Patrick's.

It would be so easy for her to drive to the bed and breakfast where he was staying. To open his door and slide into bed with him.

She could go back to pretending that everything was fine, that the smile on her lips was real. She could drive down Route 16 and ask him to forgive her. She could put their family back together again.

So why didn't she?

She closed her eyes. Because she would be lying. To her daughter. To her lover.

To herself.

She looked up at the sound of a car pulling into her mom's driveway. Her pulse beat a little faster at the thought of it being Patrick. She supposed that was a good sign—her body remembered how to feel even if the rest of her didn't.

But it wasn't Patrick. All the air left her lungs and she swallowed, trying to squelch the rising emotions that swelled at the sight of her second dad.

Thomas Carreau.

Melanie's dad and the man who'd helped raise her after her father had hightailed it to Idaho when she'd been about six.

She wanted to run out into his arms. She wanted to hear him laugh and call her Samsquatch or one of the other terrible nicknames he was forever coming up with for her and Melanie.

But instead, she sat unmoving as he climbed the front porch and walked into her mother's house without knocking.

Because he and Nancy had long ago become close friends—enough that her daughter noticed and knew about "Grammy and Thomas time".

Sam was happy for her mom. She deserved someone to make her happy.

But Sam had been avoiding seeing Thomas since she'd come home. Had left the house the moment her mom mentioned he might come by. Had avoided any chance of running into him.

Because she wasn't ready yet. She didn't know if she'd ever be.

Except that he was here now and there was no more running.

"Hey, Nattie Bear."

"Hi, Mr. Thomas," came Natalie's response.

"Where's Grammy?"

"In the bathroom. She had a sour tummy from all the cookie dough."

Sam smiled. Leave it to Natalie to share information that she was reasonably certain—no matter how close Nan and Thomas were—her mom would not want shared.

"Whatcha making?"

The exchange was normal. Completely ordinary. The kind of conversation that a grandfather would have with a granddaughter.

Except that Thomas would never have grandkids now.

"When my Melanie and your mommy were little, they used to bake chocolate chip cookies every Friday night and watch *Mystery Science Theater 3000*."

"What's that?"

"A show about a guy trapped on a space station with two robots forced to watch bad B movies for the rest of his life."

Natalie laughed. "That sounds awful. TV in the old days must have really sucked."

It was Thomas's turn to laugh quietly. "Don't underestimate it. There were some quality shows back in the dark ages of the 1980s."

"Did you have electricity when mommy was growing up?"

"Of course we did. It was twenty some odd years ago, not last century. Well, I suppose it was last century. Anyway, yes, we had power and television and phones. Life wasn't so different then."

"But you didn't have iTunes. You had to walk to the store for music."

"Yes, and don't forget about barefoot, uphill in winter. Sheesh, kiddo, you make a man feel his years."

"Natalie, stop making Mr. Thomas feel old." Nan had finally returned. Sam caught a reflection of her kissing Thomas quickly in greeting.

Why didn't they just get married? Her mom was so damn weird.

"You can just call me Thomas," he said to Natalie.

"My mommy says I have to call adults Mr. or Ms. because I'm a kid," Natalie said.

"Then how about we just let it be our secret?"

"Nuh-uh. Mommy knows when I'm keeping secrets."

"Yeah, well, Mommy doesn't know everything."

Sam took a deep breath and stepped into the kitchen. "It's a Southern thing," she said when she was sure her voice wouldn't break. It did anyway. "Kids down south don't call adults by their first names. At least not the ones I've been around."

She braced for it, that shockwave of emotion crashing over Thomas's face.

It rose violently, tearing at her insides, ripping open the chest wound that ached and bled for the sister she'd lost and the daughter he'd buried.

"Hi, Samwise." His words were choked and thick.

She blinked rapidly, trying to keep the tears from cascading down her cheeks.

She failed.

And when his arms came around her, she surrendered to the wave of crushing sadness that dragged her under.

***

Natalie and her mom were making another batch of cookies. Gingerbread men this time, apparently. Sam and Thomas sat out in the sunroom. Sam was curled in one of her mom's old wicker chairs, nursing a sad cup of coffee that was neither warm nor energizing. It didn't matter. She couldn't swallow past the block in her throat.

"We were just north of Baghdad," Sam said quietly. "There hadn't been any attacks in days. We were on patrol, meeting with a local sheik, trying to see what services they needed, what we could provide."

"Did you leave the base often?" Thomas asked.

"We did. Mel was on the battalion commander's personal security detachment, and I was with public affairs." She shrugged. "We were always together. It was just like camp. Except for the explosions and all that."

Thomas smiled. "You two were always into something. You and the damn Rierson boys and the McLaurin girls."

Sam swallowed at the mention of Cass and Ashley McLaurin. She needed to go see Cass, but she hadn't really thought through everything she was going to say.

Ashley—Cass's sister—was still in Afghanistan. She didn't know how to mourn one friend while worrying for others. It was too much, too overwhelming.

Still, seeing Thomas… For a moment, the floodgates had opened and released a cascade of grief and ragged anger. And for a moment, just a moment, it had felt good to release some of the pressure hiding in that black box she tried to ignore.

"Yeah. We had some good times," she said. Because they had.

Before the war.

"She used to write home every night." A long pause as he sipped his coffee. "I would always worry when I didn't have a note. She tried to explain to me that sometimes, the phones and Internet were shut off because someone had gotten hurt or..."

"Yeah, we'd cut the communications when someone died because we don't need families finding out about things on Facebook."

He nodded, then reached for and squeezed her hand. "Thank you for telling me before the Army showed up on my doorstep."

Sam's throat closed off, and her eyes burned again. She'd violated the rules that day.

She hadn't even given it a second thought. She'd been numb, dead inside when she'd picked up the phone in the signal officer's office that was on the exemption list and placed the call.

"Your mom stayed with me the whole time." His voice cracked a little. "It was the hardest day of my life. But couldn't you have gotten into trouble?"

Her throat was tight, locked shut, making it difficult to speak, to breathe. "Sometimes, breaking the rules is the right thing to do."

"Yeah, well, don't go breaking any more rules for me. Melanie wouldn't want you to get in trouble for her."

Sam smiled. "No, she'd be mad at me for getting into trouble without her."

"Yeah, she would, wouldn't she." Thomas chuckled. "I wonder where Nan and Natalie went off to?"

She frowned. "Mom said she was running into town for ice cream. Who eats ice cream in December in Maine?"

"Ah, everyone that I know. Ice cream isn't seasonal. Except for peppermint stick."

"You know you can't find that down in Texas. Not the good stuff anyway. Just some crappy brand made with corn syrup. It's so nasty."

"Weren't you going to take Natalie to finish Christmas shopping today?"

She glanced at the old clock on the beam above them. "I was thinking about it…"

"Well if you go, keep an eye on the weather. There's a nasty storm coming in. Lake effect snow."

"That's what I'm hearing. We might wait until tomorrow, honestly." She looked up, daring to meet his eyes. "How have you been? With everything?"

He scrubbed his hand over his scruffy grey beard, then leaned forward, folding his hands together. "When I lost Mel's mom, I thought it was the worst thing I'd ever go through. I was wrong." He looked up at her. "There's a word for when a man loses his wife. Or a wife loses a husband. There's no word for what I am now. Orphan parent is the closest thing I can come up with." He shifted a little. "But I'll get through it. You just try to keep going, try not to think about it too much because the sadness… Man, the sadness is like quicksand. It'll suck you down before you even realize you're sinking."

Sam looked away. "Yeah." It was all she could manage.

Thomas sighed heavily. "So what are you and your mom doing this week? And where's your other half?"

Sam bit her lips, wishing at that moment that Thomas wasn't as close with her mother as he was. But he knew Patrick. Knew that he'd been there from the start and raised Natalie like his own.

Knew that he was currently missing from the picture.

And Sam didn't have a good explanation for it. She couldn't put a name to the lack inside her. To the emptiness that was so deep and so dark that it felt like no light would ever penetrate it.

Someone told her that shadows were a good thing because it proved the light existed, that it was as real as whatever lurked in the shadows.

But when there was no light, there was nothing to push back the darkness. It just kept coming and coming until it overwhelmed its prey, dragging it down, further from the light.

"We're taking some time off," she said after a moment, when she realized she hadn't answered him.

Thomas said nothing for so long, Sam dared to finally look up. "You know, when I came home from Vietnam, I thought I was going to be so happy. I was alive. I'd made it. I had a wife to come home to." He paused, his gaze going to a memory decades in the past. "But that didn't happen. It was… Things didn't feel right. At the time, I thought it was because of all the bullshit we had to endure. People calling us baby killers and murderers." He rubbed his eyes behind his coke-bottle glasses. "But after a while I realized that it wasn't the public's problem. It was mine."

Sam listened intently. There was no public antiwar sentiment to make her feel like this. No, the problem was strictly hers. A problem that defied explanation.

"What did you do?"

"Self-medicated for a long time. Melanie's mother left me for a while. Was hooked on heroin for a while."

Sam frowned. "Heroin is some pretty heavy stuff." She never would have guessed that Thomas had been an addict.

"Started smoking opium while I was in Vietnam. Bunch of us did. And let me tell you, that is a habit that you never quit. Every day I wake up and have to remind myself why I'm not chasing the dragon today." He paused for a long moment. "And then I woke up one day, no idea where I was or what I'd been doing for the last year. Checked myself into a VA rehab center."

"Mel's mom took you back?"

"After a while. Took me a long time to unpack all my shit from the war." He leaned back in his chair. "So whatever is going on with you or with him, give it time. You just got home. Don't make any decisions right now because you think things are going to be this way forever." He hesitated a moment. "If you're not talking to someone, you should."

She closed her eyes, unable to find the words she needed. How to explain the fear that threatened to choke her when she even thought about what to say, how to say it?

He shifted, pointing his finger at her. "It feels like it will but it won't be. This, I promise you." He stood. "But pretending that everything will get better if you just try harder isn't the answer, Sammy. Believe me, I tried it. Sometimes, the hardest thing in the world to do is admit that your stuff is too much for you to deal with on your own."

Chapter Six

It was almost noon when he woke up.

His heart slammed against his ribs, his blood pounded in his ears as the panic receded, leaving him in a cold sweat.

The nightmare slipped through his fingers, leaving nothing but the echo of fear and terror. He frowned, tracing his thoughts, trying to remember what he'd been dreaming about and finding nothing but empty grey trails that led to dead ends.

He didn't have nightmares often. He couldn't say what triggered them.

But waking up in a strange bed in a strange room that felt a hell of a lot colder than it had when he'd crashed earlier was a way to do it.

He picked up his phone, about to call Sam when he saw her text:

Big storm coming in. Not going Christmas shopping.

From two hours ago.

Damn, he must have been tired. He never slept during the day. At least not for more than a few minutes at his desk before he got up and started slogging through the caseload yet again.

He dropped his booted feet to the floor and cradled his head in his hands. He had the start of a massive headache. That always happened when he pulled twenty-four hour duty, too.

Except he'd slept on the plane up. He shouldn't be this tired.

He palmed the phone and tapped out a message on the touch screen. *What are you doing for dinner?*

He supposed he could drive back out to Nancy's house. Not give Sam the chance to avoid him. Maybe if he hadn't given her space in the first place, they wouldn't be in this situation.

He snorted. Yeah, he should have gone all eight–hundred-pound gorilla on her. Because women totally thought cavemen were sexy.

He shook his head. He'd backed off when she'd clearly needed him to.

He remembered feeling off-kilter the first time he'd come home from war. But that was three tours ago. Now, he was used to it—and those strange feelings were nothing but a distant memory.

Still. He'd thought giving her space had been the right thing to do.

What the hell was he doing? He hadn't flown all the way to Maine to sit in a rented room with his daughter and the woman he still loved a few miles away.

"Now, that's a good use of airline miles," he muttered.

He stripped off his clothes and stepped into the tiny shower. He wasn't sure it was actually big enough for a hobbit, but he managed to get everything reasonably clean before damn near busting his ass on the bare floor.

Clearly, someone was new at the bed and breakfast thing because there was one hand towel and a tiny bath towel. He supposed it could be worse. He could be drying off with a washcloth.

He scrubbed his hands over his face then dug through his overnight bag for clothes.

And discovered that he had nothing to wear. Literally.

He sighed heavily. "And this is what packing while drunk gets you."

"Do you always talk to yourself?"

The door to his room eased open, and he spun around. Sam stood in the doorway, arms folded over her chest. Her chestnut hair was pinned to the top of her head, her cheeks flushed.

But it was her eyes that he noticed. In the deep blue eyes, he saw a spark of life that he hadn't seen in…since before she deployed. The emptiness was still there, the darkness still filling them.

It was a spark. A small one.

But it was there.

He dragged the tiny towel over his hips. "Doesn't this place have locks?"

She shrugged. "Why are you naked?"

"Isn't that a question normally reserved for Natalie?"

Sam's eyes sparkled. "You're the one standing there in a towel."

He ran his tongue over his teeth. "So I didn't really pack the right clothes for the trip."

Her lips almost twitched. "Did you forget underwear, too?"

A flush crawled up his neck. "Maybe."

"Were you drunk when you packed?"

The flush got a little hotter. "Maybe."

She shook her head slowly. "So what do you have?"

He laid everything out on the bed. "A grand total of one sock, one pair of long john bottoms, a T-shirt and a toothbrush. No toothpaste." He finally looked up at her. "Why are you here, Sam?"

The wariness was instantly back, her eyes shuttering closed. "You didn't answer my text," she said quietly.

"The phone still works."

She looked down at her booted feet. "I figured it was easier to talk to you in person. You flew all the way here and all that."

He looked at her for a long moment. A thousand ideas and harebrained schemes raced through his brain. She was here. They were alone.

Hell, he was already naked.

And hello, didn't his body like the scenic detour his brain had decided to take.

He swallowed and grabbed his pants off the floor.

He met her gaze just as the fan kicked on in the small heater.

He dropped the towel.

And refused to look away as her gaze dropped down his body and back up again. He stood there, naked and exposed and completely at her mercy.

He wondered if she knew that she could ask him anything at that moment and he'd probably do it.

Her nostrils flared ever so slightly. Her eyes darkened. Just a little.

It was the only sign that him standing there naked sparked any kind of reaction in her. But she didn't move. And wasn't that hell on the ego?

"I've got to go buy some clothes," he said, dragging his pants over his hips.

"Going commando?"

"Does that get you horny, baby?" Her lips twitched at the cheesy line from *Austin Powers*. A thousand small reactions but they added up to convincing him that he had a chance to fix this. A chance to reach her in whatever darkness had pulled her away from him and drag her back to him. Back to them. "I don't really have many options right now, do I? Not with the storm coming in. And I have no earthly idea where a laundromat is around here." He frowned. "I should probably know this but I'm drawing a complete blank. Where the hell can I get clothes?"

"There's a small trading post down the road in Greenville or you can ride to Wal-Mart in Newport."

"Isn't Newport like an hour from here?" He usually let her drive when they came home. Their visits hadn't been so long that he'd learned his way around without GPS.

"Forty minutes."

"Seems like I should get what I need closer to home tonight. Or I could just wait until the storm passes."

She shook her head slowly. "You don't want to be riding around without underwear or socks. If you go off the road, you'll freeze off some of your bits and pieces."

He lifted one brow. "Sounds like you might be concerned with my bits and pieces."

She lifted one shoulder. "They're nice bits and pieces."

He grinned and said nothing for a moment, not pressing his advantage in the opening she'd just left him.

He wanted her. He'd love nothing more than to lay her down in that bed and feel her body surround him. He wanted to savor the heat from her skin, the soft, silken wetness between her thighs. He wanted to feel her gasp as he slid inside her. Wanted to feel her breath on his ear, her nails in his back.

He wanted that and so much more.

But looking at her standing near the door, seeing the faint hints of awareness sparking in her eyes, he had an idea.

It was a terrible, terrible idea.

It was dark and wicked and would either work beautifully or ruin everything.

Chapter Seven

He'd asked if she'd go with him. To keep him from getting lost and dying in a snow bank on the side of the road.

She'd thought about saying no. About heading back to her mother's house and finishing decorating the Christmas cookies with Natalie and her mom.

But Natalie was being strangely clingy with her grandmother, so Sam let her be when she'd told her mom she was going to go talk to Patrick.

"Good," she'd said simply. "Natalie and I will stay out of trouble. Promise."

She'd frowned. "What does that mean, Mom?"

"It means that she'll wear a helmet if we go out on Thomas's snowmobile later today."

Sam had glanced at her watch. "It's already one. It'll be dark soon."

Darkness came early up in the great north woods. It had taken her a day to remember that when she'd gone into the grocery store in broad daylight and come out in pitch darkness. At four p.m.

"Snowmobiles have headlights."

So her mother was making cookies, her daughter was being exceptionally cooperative, and Sam was shopping for clothes with a man she was leaving. She'd sent her mom a text to let her know she was going to be late.

She'd gotten no response, which meant that Natalie and her mom were probably passed out from sugar overdose.

Now, she meandered around the men's department, looking at sweaters, turtlenecks, and other articles of clothing suitable for surviving the Maine winter.

"I can't believe how much flannel is still being sold in this state."

She turned to see him standing behind her. He wore a charcoal grey turtleneck beneath a red-checkered flannel shirt.

"You look like an L.L. Bean commercial."

"I feel like an escapee from a Pearl Jam concert circa 1994."

"Pearl Jam concert goers did not wear turtlenecks with their flannel, and they damn sure didn't tuck them in." She tipped her chin at him. For the first time since she'd come home, she smiled and it felt normal. "Flannel is an incredibly functional fabric, especially at ten below."

"Yes, but it went out of style in the rest of the country somewhere around 1996."

"So did mom jeans, but you still see those up here, too."

He glanced around. "Really? There are pleated jeans for sale?"

"Why do you know that pleated jeans are mom jeans?" She held up one hand. "Never mind, don't answer that." She paused, taking in the entire selection of clothing he'd picked out. "If flannel is so nineties why are you wearing it?"

"Because this is the warmest thing I've tried on. Nerdy turtleneck included."

She shot him a baleful look. "You realize that men are supposed to run hot. It's the women folk who are supposed to be cold."

"Are you calling me a woman? Because I might have to take offense to that." He took a single step closer, blocking her from the view of the rest of the store. "I assure you, flannel or not"—he leaned closer, until his breath slid across her ear—"I'm all man, baby."

The corniness of his line did nothing to undermine the heat of his touch. She closed her eyes as his lips barely brushed the outside of her ear. A sliver of pleasure shivered over her skin. Her breath caught in her throat as she waited for the sensation of his lips against her skin in the place he loved to touch her.

And then he was gone, his warmth replaced by the cool circulating air.

He untucked the shirt. "I'll be in the changing room." He plucked a blue and grey sweater from a table.

And left her there.

She stood for a moment, watching his retreating back before he disappeared behind the curtain.

She narrowed her eyes. He'd done that on purpose. He'd stepped too close, teased her with one of the things he knew drove her crazy.

And then he'd simply stopped.

She breathed deeply, wishing for a moment that things were normal. That the feelings he'd just sparked inside her weren't fleeting.

That the flash of desire hadn't already faded, dissipating into the darkness inside her.

She wanted to feel it again.

Because in that single instance, she'd felt real. She'd felt whole.

She'd felt like her again.

She stuffed her hands inside her jacket pockets and walked toward the dressing room.

"Hey, Sam?"

"Yeah?"

"Can you come check something out for me?"

She paused. "Is this going to get us arrested?" Silence greeted her question. "Are you done trying things on?"

More silence.

"Patrick?"

Nothing.

She reached for the curtain.

At the same time he stepped out.

Wearing nothing but silkies—white ones that clung to his skin like some kind of superhero leotard, outlining every hard line and yes, every part of his body. He'd pulled them up high so the waist was up to his chest.

"What do you think?"

She covered her mouth and tried not to laugh. "That looks painful," she said when she was sure she wouldn't choke.

"Well, it's not like I've got any future kids to worry about."

The minute the words were out of his mouth, they both sobered. It was instant and simultaneous.

She hesitated, only a moment, turning his words over and inspecting them and coming up with no easy answers. "What are you talking about?"

"Nothing. Never mind. It was a bad joke."

He disappeared into the changing room, leaving her feeling completely alone. He was two feet away and he might as well have been on the other side of the world.

"Patrick?"

He didn't answer. She didn't expect him to.

She stood on the other side of the curtain. It would be so easy to step inside. To cross that threshold and wrap her arms around him and ask him to help her.

I'm sorry. But the words wouldn't form in her throat.

Because there was so much for her to be sorry for, and she didn't know where to start.

But she was tired. So tired of feeling like a dead thing going through the motions.

She stood there, on the other side of the curtain, unable to move, unwilling to leave.

Stuck. Just like always.

And she was so damn tired of being stuck.

***

He felt the air move across his bare back a moment before she stepped into the changing room.

His pants hung open. His shirt was in his hands.

Her coat was unzipped, revealing the red fleece vest she wore over god only knew how many layers of clothing.

"Sam." Her name was a whisper. A plea.

A moment before he would have loved for her to step into this dressing room with him. Would have enjoyed standing a little too close. Running his lips down the edge of her ear the way he knew she liked.

But right then, he needed some space. He wasn't ready to have the conversation she probably expected the moment she stepped into that changing room.

"I'm finished," he said. "I'll get dressed and we can go."

Her eyes betrayed her. He saw the unasked question looking back at him.

It was his own fault. He shouldn't have opened his damn mouth.

But he'd been teasing her, and she'd been responding. Slowly, like a flower first stretching in springtime, he'd seen her, really her, not the shadow that had been masquerading as her.

Then he'd slipped up.

He hadn't meant to tell her he couldn't have kids.

But there was no taking those words back now.

And she wasn't about to let it go. "What did you mean?" A hushed question.

He closed his eyes. Dropped his hands to his sides. "There was a mortar attack."

"You never told me."

He swallowed hard. "Since we weren't married, they didn't notify you." He looked away. "I didn't know how to tell you. I didn't want you to worry." He paused, searching for the words to explain what happened. It was hard, so damn hard to put something like that into words. "I got hit. Some things didn't make it out okay."

She said nothing for a long moment. "I never noticed."

He smiled sadly. "It's not like you spend a lot of time inspecting my bits and pieces these days."

The truth. Not meant to be unkind. It was a painful truth. Then again, weren't all truths painful? Things had started changing between them long before her deployment. After his last tour, he'd just been happy to be home.

He hadn't noticed the distance growing between them. Not until she'd deployed two weeks after he'd come back.

They'd literally done a battle hand-off with Natalie's schoolwork and contact information, and she'd been gone.

They'd spent almost two years apart between their two back-to-back deployments.

He swallowed. It was too much time lost, too many hours spent working and not nearly enough time tending to the thing that had drawn them together to begin with. They'd simply grown apart, and now? Now here they were, trying to figure out who these two strangers in a room were.

Strangers who shared the only daughter Patrick would ever have.

"You could have told me," she said quietly.

He shrugged and the gesture felt empty. "It never really came up. Hard to fit 'oh, by the way I got blown up and my balls got rewired' with 'where's your spaghetti recipe,' you know?"

Her response was not what he expected.

She laughed. She covered her mouth and laughed until she doubled over.

Patrick stood there, not sure what to do or what he'd said that was so damn funny.

"I guess my emergency neutering is funny. Okay then."

She straightened, tears running down her cheeks. "I'm sorry. It's not funny. It's just the way you said it and…" She doubled over again, laughing until she slid down the wall and covered her face with both hands.

He watched her, amazed at the sound of her laughter. In that moment, he realized that she hadn't really laughed in… He couldn't remember the last time she'd laughed like this. Slowly a matching smile spread over his lips, and he stood there and simply savored the moment.

It was something he'd forgotten. Something that had slipped away as the distance between them had grown wider and deeper.

He'd enjoyed making her laugh once upon a time. A thousand memories surfaced and tormented him with the pleasure of her laugh. God but he loved the way she used to smile.

She swiped at her eyes, looking up at him from the changing room floor. "I'm sorry."

"For laughing at my neutering or my being neutered?" he asked lightly, holding his hand out to help her up.

"Both." Her palm slid against his.

He gave a gentle tug and she was on her feet, close enough that he could see the moisture sparkling in her eyes. "It's been so long since I heard you laugh," he murmured.

Her mouth was a breath from his. Warm air brushed against his skin. He could almost taste the laugh on her lips.

She smiled ruefully. "There hasn't been a lot to laugh about lately."

Her hands came up, braced against his skin. Her palms were cool on his bare shoulders, sending a shiver through his veins. It had been so long since he'd touched her. Since she'd touched him. This. This was opportunity.

In a perfect world, he could kiss her then. Rock her world and remind her of all the things that had once been right between them.

But this wasn't a perfect world. This was a flawed and damaged world.

But it wasn't hopeless. No, he hadn't given up hope yet.

He stood there for a moment, his eyes locked with hers. Her lips were parted, the slightest space. He wanted to nibble on her there, to suck gently until she sighed.

Instead he lifted his hand. Ran his thumb gently, so gently over her bottom lip. She was soft and smooth and warm. It was meant to tease them both. It was meant to control the situation, to keep himself from deviating from his game plan of trying to lure her out of the darkness and shadows where she'd been for too long.

Instead, Sam took over.

She'd never been a passive lover. Her tongue slid over the bottom of his thumb. A gentle rasp of heat on heat. It was warm and wet against the roughness of his skin.

So long. So fucking long since he'd touched her. That single gesture drove his resolve away, turning his plan on its head and sending him headlong into the abyss of sensation. She slipped her tongue around the tip, swirling a teasing pattern, her eyes never leaving his. She sucked him further into the warmth of her mouth and he gave himself over to the sensation.

This. This was always good between them. This was always right.

He backed her up against the wall, his thumb slipping out of her mouth with a soft pop. It was just them, alone in the bright lights of the changing room. Their breath mixing as they stood, his bare skin pressing against her clothed form.

He lowered his forehead to hers. Stroked her cheek gently with his thumb.

"I miss you."

Chapter Eight

Sam waited outside for him to finish checking out. Snow was already falling, big fat flakes that stuck to everything. A gust of wind from Moosehead Lake sent it swirling around her. She huddled deeper in her jacket.

In the end, he'd decided on a couple of pairs of heavy socks, a couple of wool sweaters, and two pairs of jeans, along with, yes, a flannel shirt. And somehow, damn it, Patrick made flannel look sexy.

He wasn't exactly a flannel kind of guy. He wore expensive button-down shirts and loafers. He drank aged scotch and listened to classical music and pretended to be a cultural omnivore when he was in public. She knew his secrets, though, knew he listened to heavy metal when he was at the gym.

And she remembered how to make him beg when they were alone.

But the flannel shirt he wore now beneath the heavy Patagonia jacket made him look more rugged. Less polished.

Less like Patrick the soldier and more like someone else.

Someone else who had just pinned her to the wall in a changing room and sent her blood spiking.

It was that Patrick that she was drawn to now. That Patrick who instead of kissing her had simply stood for a moment, his heat and warmth surrounding her, urging her closer, urging her to *feel* for the first time in forever.

She didn't know what to do with all the feelings he'd aroused in her. There was an ache deep in her belly that made her crave more. An ache she'd once not hesitated to satiate with him.

So why was she hesitating now? Why hadn't she leaned forward and kissed him when he'd been so close? God, but she'd loved seeing his eyes go dark when she'd run her tongue over his thumb. She'd pushed him closer to the edge. Closer to taking.

But he was too much of a good man to do that.

She knew that.

And yet, standing there in the swirling snow, waiting for him to step outside, she felt the darkness stalking her. The numbing sensation was wrapping around her, chasing away the awareness and arousal he'd sparked in her and leaving her with nothing but the memory.

She was clawing her way toward the surface at the bottom of a long dark well. She could see the light. She wanted to be in the light.

But it was so far away.

The bell on the door behind her jingled as he stepped into the cold.

"Hey." His voice was thick. His breath froze on the air in front of him. He looked up at the darkening sky. "Looks like we didn't miss the storm."

She nodded toward the rental car. "Does that thing have four-wheel drive? It's about to get nasty."

He looked at the sedan. "I have no idea. Do cars come with four-wheel drive up here? Are they specially made for living in the great north woods?"

She shook her head. "We should get going before the roads get worse."

"We'll be able to get home, right?"

She smiled. "The road crews up here are pretty busy in the winter. The main roads are usually fine."

"I hear a but in there."

"But we probably don't want to tempt fate. We'll end up sleeping in the parking lot 'til morning if there's an accident."

He stepped closer to her, his coat rustling in the falling darkness. "I'd keep you warm."

She lowered her eyes from the temptation in his. "I have no doubt."

They walked in silence to the car.

"I cannot get over how cold it is up here. How on earth did you grow up and not freeze to death?"

"Listen, Florida boy, not all of us are used to sunny weather and sandy beaches all the time."

It felt good, teasing him. To have such a normal conversation that felt like things weren't so irreparably damaged between them. Like maybe there was a chance she wasn't completely broken.

Maybe she could hold on to this normalcy. Maybe she could claim this moment and cherish it.

Maybe she could hold on long enough to climb out of the well.

The snow was falling faster now, looking like the streaks of stars when the *Millennium Falcon* jumped to light speed. Visibility sucked and was likely to get worse. "So, want to tell me about when you got hurt?"

"There's not much to tell. Shrapnel in a very special place, the docs said things were probably destroyed, and wow, isn't this a fun and entertaining conversation."

"Probably destroyed?"

His knuckles whitened where he gripped the steering wheel. "I could have gone back to Germany and had surgery to try and save the boys." He released a deep breath.

It was not an easy conversation to have.

It was even harder now.

She should have let it go. She should walk away from the edge of the argument teetering just in front of them. But she couldn't. "Why didn't you?"

"Because it felt wrong to try and keep my balls in good working order when other guys were losing arms and legs and eyesight." He ground his teeth. "And I had Natalie," he whispered. "It sounds fucked up, but I wasn't overly worried about it. I didn't die, the important thing still works, and it just seemed more important to stay in the fight."

She watched him while he spoke. Watched the tension crank higher and higher until his hands looked like they were going to break the steering wheel.

"I thought I was okay when I made it home. But I wasn't." He swallowed hard. "Spent some time talking to a counselor off post," he said cautiously.

She looked down at her hands. "You never mentioned that."

"It's a hard thing to admit that you're not okay. Everyone pretends that everything is fine when it fucking isn't." He rubbed his hand over his mouth. "I got my head straight and, well, it never came up. Maybe it should have. Maybe if I'd been honest with you about what I'd gone through…" He stopped suddenly.

"What?" A broken whisper.

"Maybe you wouldn't have felt so alone. Like you were the only one who'd ever had trouble coming home." He brought their vehicle to a stop as the taillights of the tanker truck in front of him lit up. Finally, he glanced over at her. "Maybe you wouldn't have felt like leaving was the only option."

***

The admission hurt: it was staring at the reality of his own failure. He'd tried to be strong, tried to keep from laying his own burdens on her. In doing so, he'd left her alone when she needed someone, anyone to lean on.

He'd never thought that she'd leave him. Maybe it was his own naiveté that they'd get through the war and figure things out on the other side. He'd always respected what she stood for, what she needed. He'd never pressured her to get married. He knew how important it was to her to keep her name, to feel like she could do things on her own. She was stubborn like that.

She'd been burned badly by Natalie's biological father. He remembered the first time he met her.

He'd been at BookPeople in Austin, one of his favorite haunts when he wasn't working.

He'd seen her standing in the politics section. She'd looked adorable in a pale blue and white sundress. It had taken him a minute to recognize her from work. A lot of military women looked completely different out of uniform, and Sam was no different. Her hair had been down, spilling down her back and brushing over her shoulders.

Then she'd glanced toward him, and he'd seen the tears streaming down her face.

Before he'd seen those tears, he'd been on the fence about approaching. About saying hi. But those tears had punched him in the gut. She was always so strong at work. So confident.

In that moment, he'd made a decision that had changed the course of both their lives.

He'd approached cautiously. "Whoever it is, I'm sure it's nothing a good kick in the balls can't solve."

She'd been embarrassed. She'd tried to shrug off his concern.

But he'd convinced her to cross the street with him and let him buy her lunch.

She'd confided in him that day. Told him about the boyfriend who hadn't just run out on her, but had emptied her bank accounts and run up her credit cards first. He'd left her broke and betrayed everything Sam thought that she'd had with him.

They'd been dating for a month when she'd dropped a land mine on both of them.

She was pregnant. And since they hadn't yet made love, she hadn't had to tell him that it wasn't his.

God, he could still see her face when she'd told him the news. She'd braced for him to walk out on her.

But he hadn't. And over the years, he'd gotten used to the careful balancing of her independence with her relationship with him.

"I never pushed you on the paperwork for Natalie because I never thought I'd have to," he said now, sitting on a snow-covered road behind a stopped tractor-trailer in the middle of central Maine. "And we managed to make this stuff work without being married." He looked at her then, and crossed the boundary he'd never broken with them before. "I get that you have your stuff. We all do. But I never thought you'd take her away from me. I never thought through what would happen the day you decided you'd had enough. I loved you—I still love you—and I always thought that was enough."

"You make it sound so simple." A ragged whisper. "It's not."

"Yes, actually it is." He forced his voice to remain level. To stay calm and not shout at her that she was destroying everything he loved in this world. "That this isn't just about Natalie, but about the life we've built together. This is about you and it's about me and about us. And things are a little fucked up right now but you're doing exactly what you've always been afraid I would do to you. You're running away."

Her mouth opened, then closed again. He wanted her to fight, to deny what he said. To tell him he was imagining things. But she didn't. She simply bit her lips together and looked away, avoiding his eyes.

It was an old familiar story in the military. Too many soldiers deployed to return home to find their spouses shacked up with someone else. Too many soldiers strayed while they were deployed, figuring deployment meant they didn't have to honor their marriage vows.

He'd done neither. He'd always believed she would do the same.

But now the ugly suspicion settled around his heart, and he had to ask. Had to know. "Is there someone else?" he asked flatly.

Better to excise the wound than to let it fester.

"No." She turned away, looking out into the swirling snow. "There's no one else."

He dropped his head back against the headrest, lashing at his temper that was fraying at the edge. "Then explain to me what happened, Sam. Because if you're going to destroy everything we built together, I deserve to know why."

She flinched when he spoke. His deceptively calm words hurt. He knew that. Could see the evidence on her face.

She didn't answer. Not right away. He waited patiently, let the silence stand between them, growing until it was a live thing, crackling with energy that snapped and hissed.

"Because I don't feel anything anymore." Words like shattered glass. "Because nothing between us feels alive. It feels like we're going through the motions, waiting for bedtime when we can both roll over and pretend to be asleep." She finally dared to look at him. "I can't pretend to feel something that isn't there anymore. I can't do that to Natalie." She looked away again. "And you deserve someone who can make you laugh. Someone who isn't broken." Her voice cracked on the last sentence.

He glanced at the truck in front of them. Let her words sink in. Weighed them against the woman he knew. The woman he loved.

She was lost, utterly and completely lost. He remembered feeling that way, feeling the need to hide it from the world. Being unable to see his way out of the darkness that surrounded him.

And he'd missed the signs in her. For a thousand pointless reasons, he'd missed them.

He'd left her alone in the dark.

Because he could do nothing less, he reached for her then. Cradled her cheek until she turned to face him. "You're not broken, Sam." He gave up on his plan. Abandoned it in the nearest snow bank, needing only to be there for her. To hold her and let her know he was there. At that moment and forever. He'd never leave her alone again. He brushed his lips against hers. "You went to war. You lost people you care about." A gentle nudge. "You're not broken. You're just different. We're all different when we come home."

She closed her eyes, avoiding his.

It was a long moment before she nuzzled his hand with her cheek. "I don't want to be different." Tired words filled with sadness. She leaned in, resting her forehead against his. "I want to feel normal again." She pressed her lips to his. Slid her tongue against his. A hesitant touch. "Make me feel again, Patrick."

And he was lost.

Chapter Nine

It started as something gentle. Something hesitant.

And then it wasn't. Not gentle. It was not tame or timid or questioning.

It burned her down to the roots of her soul. It touched something deep and dark and hidden.

Something she'd thought was long since dead and buried and gone.

His tongue slid against hers, stroking to life the very sensations she thought she'd never feel again.

It was electric, the feel of his mouth against hers. The scrape of stubble against her chin, the taste of him. The smell of his skin.

He nipped her. Pinched her bottom lip between his teeth and sucked it. And she sighed at the pleasure, at the raw ache his taste and touch aroused in her, pushing aside the darkness that haunted her.

She felt him. Felt everything. The heat of his skin. The warmth that drew her closer. That made her want to crawl into his lap and unzip his pants and push up that damned flannel shirt until they were skin to skin and there was nothing between them but sweat and heat.

One hand slid down her side. Tugged at her fleece and...

"Dear lord," he muttered against her lips. "How many layers of clothing do you have on under this thing?"

She smiled. "You weren't wondering why I wasn't cold?"

"Well, you'd be a champ at strip poker right about now," he said dryly.

Then his fingers found her skin, and she was no longer thinking.

He traced the very tips of his fingers over her belly. Light, feathery strokes that made her skin quiver. She gasped when he slipped them higher, finding the swell of her breast. Every cell in her body was alert to his touch, anticipating the next stroke of his fingers.

He lifted his mouth from hers. Pressed his tongue to the corner of her lips before nipping her there.

Then he paused, pressing his cheek to hers. Just for a moment, the world fell away, and he was there, holding her, cradling her, reminding her of everything that was still good between them.

It was a moment before she felt it. His breath teasing the sensitive flesh around her ear. A quiet huff of air against her skin. Her body tensed, waiting for his touch, his tongue.

A delicious torment. An old familiar heat slid through her veins, warming her, pulling her out of the darkness at the bottom of the well.

In the silence of heated desire, of hushed passion, she heard it.

Someone gently rapping on the driver's side window.

She pulled back, seeing the wanting smile on Patrick's lips. "Someone's timing sucks."

He released her and her skin protested the loss of his touch. She shivered as he rolled the window down.

"Well," Garrett said, leaning down on the side of the car, "it's certainly awkward meeting you like this."

Sam offered a guilty half smile. "I was going to call."

"Sure. I get that all the time. Anyway, you two probably need to turn around. Bad accident up ahead, and the road is going to be closed until we get it cleaned up. With the storm coming in, you're not getting by any time soon."

"Where are we supposed to go?" Sam asked. "I don't think this thing has four-wheel drive."

"Well, maybe if you two weren't making out like a couple of horny teenagers, you'd have paid better attention to the roads." He pulled a single key off his loop. "My parents' house is about a half a mile that way." He pointed back the way they'd come.

She swallowed the resurgent lump in her throat. Her mom had told her about Garrett's parents last year when it happened. She'd been deployed.

She'd sent flowers from Iraq because it was the only thing she could think to do from half a world away.

Patrick accepted the key.

"I'll find you tomorrow with the key."

"Sure." He stepped back away from the car, using his flashlight to guide them as they turned around. "Now get your asses out of the storm before I have to dig you out in the spring."

It was easy enough to find the Rierson's house. Set back in an old field, the driveway that led up to the old log cabin had recently been plowed.

The silence between them was quiet. Comfortable.

And filled with needy tension.

They walked into the old house and Sam felt an aching sense of the familiar twisted now with age and experience. It was the same and not the same. It felt smaller, somehow, from the house she remembered as a teen.

She paused in the entryway as Patrick closed the door behind them. For a moment, the world fell away, taking the darkness and the sadness and the emptiness with it. Leaving a warmth, a sense of being home in its place. Funny. She hadn't spent time in this house in years but it felt...good.

She glanced over at Patrick. Saw him watching her. Standing close, too close and not close enough. She met his gaze and in that moment, realized with aching clarity that they were alone.

Really alone.

Her mouth went dry.

He waited. In the shadows and the snow by the door, he waited.

She wanted him to move into her space and kiss her and make her feel alive again.

But she knew this man. Despite the chasm that had grown between them, she knew him.

And she knew that he would wait. Would stand quietly by until she made that first choice.

She would never be alone.

But that first hesitant step, she had to make by herself.

He wouldn't force her.

It was one of the things she loved about him. He was steadfast and loyal and good.

And she was losing him through her own inaction.

She stood there then, taking in the sight of the man who'd stood by her the day she'd told him she was pregnant with someone else's child.

The day he'd held her hand and told her he'd always be there for her.

The day he'd gone with her into the hospital and went through labor and delivery to bring their daughter into the world.

He'd never left her alone.

Not even now when she'd left him alone in the cold and the dark.

It was a long moment. The storm whipped against the outside storm door, slamming it open, then shut and startling them both.

Shattering the moment and leaving a chill between them. She shivered at the suddenness of the feeling.

He stepped to her then, running his hands down her arms. "I'll start a fire."

She let him go because she was a coward. Because she was afraid. Afraid of what he made her feel.

Of what her life would feel like without him.

Of what her life would feel like if all the
emotions she'd locked away came tumbling out.

***

The fire was warm on his face. It penetrated the
flannel and the wool and heated his skin.

But it didn't heat the fear in the seat of his soul
that said he was losing her. That she was slipping
further away.

He'd hoped she would make that step. That
after the car and the changing room, she would trust
him enough to let him help with whatever was eating
at her.

But she hadn't moved, and it had *hurt*.

He hadn't been prepared for the hurt. He
should have expected it. He knew she didn't do
impulsive or rash. She always looked before she
leaped.

He was asking her to leap. Without saying the
words, asking her to take that step, out of the
darkness and back into the light.

And so to avoid the hurt, to avoid saying
something that would set his campaign back a dozen
lifetimes, he let her be.

He made the fire instead and hoped that maybe
this storm was a blessing in disguise. That maybe this
time alone was something they'd both needed and
hadn't realized it.

Because maybe they'd gotten so caught up with
being Captain Samantha Egan and Major Patrick
MacLean and Mommy and Daddy that they'd
forgotten how to be Sam and Patrick.

She walked up behind him. "Beer?" She held out a dark glass bottle.

"Thanks."

"I figure we'll replace it tomorrow when we find Garrett and give him the key." She sank down on the floor next to him, leaning back on the old worn couch.

"Sounds like a good plan. Did you call your mom?"

"Yeah. Natalie's being funny. She didn't even ask where we'd be."

He twisted off the cap, turning it over in his fingers before taking a long pull. "You know she called me, right?"

"Yeah, you mentioned that."

"I'm pretty sure she's conspiring to get us together," he said quietly.

"I fail to see how an eight-year-old can do that."

He shrugged. "I won't go so far as to say she's got a direct line to God, but I'll definitely give her some credit in this whole scheme. I mean we wouldn't be snowed in if she hadn't called me." He glanced over at her. The firelight danced over her skin, teasing him with orange and red and glowing shadows and light. "She's a pretty perceptive little bugger."

"You know she hasn't said a word about why we were here without you." She twisted the cap off her own beer, nestling the bottle between her bent knees. "And I wasn't ready to explain."

"What did you tell her when you left?" Because he needed to know.

"That you had to work." She lifted her gaze to his. "A convenient lie."

It was Patrick's turn to look away. To avoid the hurt that rose sudden and sharp inside him.

"She figured it out anyway," he said when he could speak.

"Yeah. She did."

They sat in silence, the fire crackling and snapping in front of them. She shifted after a bit until their shoulders were touching. Until her thighs pressed against his.

He didn't move. Didn't take advantage of her closeness.

He just savored it. Savored the fact that she was there. That she'd moved closer.

That she hadn't run away.

He'd expected her to.

"I remember the day you told me you were pregnant with her." His voice was hushed, now. Calm.

"I thought you'd leave. Any other guy would have." She looked into her beer, rubbing her thumb over the condensation. "Not my proudest moment."

"It was a pretty rough day for a month-old relationship, I'll give you that."

She glanced at him, the fire reflecting in her eyes. "Why are you so damn patient? And calm. I've never seen you not calm."

He took a long pull off his beer. "You didn't see me the day you left."

Quiet words. Filled with hurt and pain and grief.

"I spent two days at the bottom of a bottle."

"I don't think I've ever seen you drunk."

He raised his beer in mock salute. "I save getting plastered for special occasions." She snorted quietly. He looked over at her once again.

"When I came home after that last tour, I couldn't wait to see you. I was so goddamned happy to be alive." He rubbed his thumb along the edge of the label. "Part of me, though, whispered that you wouldn't stay if you knew about my accident. I was ashamed of that voice, those whispers. They weren't me. They lied." He swallowed hard. "I couldn't shut them down, though, until I recognized what they were."

* * *

She closed her eyes, letting his words sink in. Turning them over, inspecting them. Weighing them against the truth of her life for the last few months. "I couldn't—I can't—believe that I won't always feel this way." An admission laced with guilt. With fear.

He shifted then, resting his hand on the back of the sofa where they leaned against it on the floor in front of the fireplace. He brushed her hair gently away from her neck. "You can get better. This stuff— it's just post deployment stuff. You went through an incredibly dangerous experience. This—what you went through, what I went through—it took me a while to learn that it's a completely normal reaction to a completely abnormal situation."

"What if it's not?" Fear, dark and powerful, laced those words. "What if it doesn't get better? What if talking to Doc and taking meds and getting sleep—what if nothing helps?"

"What if it does?" He leaned closer then, brushing his lips against her forehead. "I'm so sorry I didn't see how hard this was for you," he whispered.

She couldn't speak. Her throat was tight, her heart pounding violently in her chest. The voice in her head told her he wouldn't—he couldn't still love her after this. But it was wrong. He was there, standing strong and steady with her, just like he always was. She just had to trust. To ignore the whispers that told her she was a broken, useless thing. That he would be better off without her.

After a moment she set her beer on the edge of the hearth. Pale golden light danced in the glass.

And then she moved. Urged his knees down and slid into his lap until she straddled him.

He froze. Unwilling to move or unable, she wasn't sure.

He set his beer down and lowered his hands to the floor. Just near her hips.

And waited.

For an explanation. For answers. For any sign that she heard what he said and believed he'd meant every word.

Neither of them were perfect. Neither of them was without sin in the decay of their relationship.

* * *

Sitting there, the woman he loved straddling his hips, her hair surrounding her face in a chestnut halo, he waited. It was the longest wait of his life but he couldn't move. Couldn't risk screwing up and shattering the tentative bridge spanning the distance between them.

Until she was ready.

And prayed that she would make the leap.

Chapter Ten

She slid her hands over his shoulders. The flannel was soft beneath her touch, the man under her palms solid and rock steady.

She ran her hands down his chest. Felt the strength and the stillness.

The anticipation.

It was a delicious thing, touching him again.

A feeling that brought things to life inside her, that terrified her.

She was afraid. Afraid of the feelings she couldn't control. Afraid that if she opened the box, she'd never get it closed again.

Afraid that if she let him in and showed him all the broken things that were left of her life from before the war, he would walk away. That he'd finally leave her alone.

To face the world without him.

She leaned closer. Inhaled the warm, spicy scent of his skin. Smelled the fire and the heat as she pressed her lips to the edge of his mouth. Flicked her tongue out to press against the seam of his lips. Felt the shudder run through him as she explored.

Knew that he wouldn't move until she was ready.

Each touch of her lips to his skin ignited a fire in her. Flicked the latch off the box and weakened her hold on the darkness inside her. It was a gamble, a risk.

She could do this. She could give in to the need, to the desire without completely losing control over everything she'd struggled to keep locked away.

A rasp of teeth against his earlobe. His hands gripped her thighs then, kneading gently. A gentle movement beneath her in the ever so slight rocking of his hips.

She wanted this. Wanted him.

Her fingers danced down his chest, flicking the buttons open on that flannel shirt. The turtleneck came untucked easily.

"I love your chest." A throaty whisper, her voice thick. She leaned down, pressing her lips to the soft hair on his stomach. He was still but the quiver beneath her lips gave away the tension he struggled to control.

She looked up at him. Loved the sight of him watching her, his eyes heavy lidded and dark. His breath came in short huffs.

Heat flooded her. She loved the idea that he was watching her. That she could use her lips and her tongue and her fingers to tease him, to touch him.

To tell him with her body what she could not speak.

She couldn't explain why she'd left. She couldn't explain to him the lack in her or find the words to describe it. Losing her best friend shouldn't have destroyed her like this. She should have been stronger, should have fought harder to keep the depression from consuming everything. Going to war should not have utterly dismantled everything she'd thought she was.

But it had. And her denial, her stubborn denial had compounded everything.

She stroked her thumb over the soft hair just above the waistband of his pants. He licked his bottom lip, his body tense.

"Sam." A plea. A prayer. Maybe both.

She nipped him there, just above his jeans. Scraped her teeth over his skin and felt his stomach jump beneath her lips. Felt the answering heat deep in her own belly.

She'd missed this. Missed touching him. Missed feeling him beneath her. Missed the pleasure of sliding her body against his.

Missed *feeling.*

She opened the button on his jeans, her eyes locked on his. Slowly, so slowly opened the zipper.

His lips parted. Anticipation. Arousal. Maybe both.

She narrowed her eyes at the slow smile that spread across his mouth. "What are you thinking?" She pressed her lips to his belly.

His lips quivered. "It's been a long time since you inspected my bits and pieces."

She swallowed hard and pushed his pants open. The tip of his erection rested against his groin. Teasing her.

It had been so long since she'd done this with him. Since she'd taken him in her mouth and tasted him.

Brought them both so much pleasure with something so simple.

She urged his pants down. He lifted his hips, and she slid them down farther, exposing the thick length of him. She hesitated, curious now that he'd brought it up.

"Here," he said. He slid her finger over the soft skin at the bottom of his sac near a rough, ragged scar.

"I wouldn't have found that," she whispered.

He shrugged. "Now you know."

There was more there. Unsaid things that could wait.

Because he was right in front of her. And she wanted to lose herself in the sensation of touching him. Of feeling his body tense when she used her mouth on him.

She watched him carefully. Lowered her lips to press a soft kiss on the tip of him where he was moist and smooth. Savored the warm smell that was uniquely and completely his.

She took him in her mouth. Sucked on him gently. Heard his shuddering sigh of relief or pleasure or both.

She cradled him where he was soft as she swirled her tongue over his length. Felt his gasp when she dragged her teeth gently over his tip before kissing him gently there once more.

He reached for her then. He urged her up until she was in his lap once more, his mouth feasting on hers. There was no restraint in his kiss now. No patience.

Only hunger. Raw and powerful and filled with needful things.

"Why am I always naked and you always have clothes on?" His words were a murmur against her mouth a moment before he feasted on her again. One hand gripped her hip as he rocked against her. Sparks simmering in her belly exploded in full-blown, wild pleasure.

Tighter. Higher. Harder. Until she thought she would snap from the pressure. "Patrick, please."

He stilled then. Cupped her cheeks and sipped at her lips. Bringing them both back from the edge of mindlessness.

Her body protested at the edge of the cliff, needing, craving the release he'd brought her so close to.

She arched against him. "Please." Her words were almost a sob. "I need you," she whispered.

***

He took his time stripping her naked. One piece of clothing at a time, inch by inch.

Felt her shiver beneath his touch as he traced the pad of his index finger over the smooth skin of her belly.

Her skin glowed in the firelight. The flames and the heat licked at her even as he used his tongue to follow his fingers. Her body was tense, her muscles tight with a lithe tension. He slipped his palms over her ribs, urging her arms up, over her head. She parted her thighs, urging him home as he leaned over her. He nuzzled her nose before lifting his hips away from the contact they both craved.

She scowled at him. "You know, for a man who hasn't been with a woman in a long, long time, you've got remarkable staying power." She arched beneath him, a beautiful, fire-licked goddess.

He smiled, trailing his fingers down the underside of her arms. Tracing the edge of her breasts. Her nipples puckered beneath his touch.

He ignored her taunt. "You're so beautiful, Samantha." He'd waited for this. Hoped for it. Hoped that it would be the miracle they needed to put their relationship back together again. This alone time, this precious moment when it could be just him and just her. The storm outside was far away.

She narrowed her eyes at him. "I may stop speaking to you if you don't get your damn pants completely off and…"

He covered her mouth with his, cutting off her words with a kiss meant to drive them both closer to the edge. "I want to go slow. I want to remember every detail."

"Can we do the remember-every-detail thing in a few minutes?"

He splayed his palm over her belly when she moved to sit up. He shook his head. "My turn," he whispered before placing a kiss at the soft center of her belly.

She bowed her back off the blanket with a quiet gasp.

It was good, so damned good to see her like this.

The fact that he'd almost lost her made it all the more sweet.

He nuzzled her belly for a moment, then traced his fingers beneath the edge of her panties.

She made a sexy sound deep in her throat.

She wasn't used to lying back. She was not a submissive, passive lover. She took as much as she received. He knew that, and he damn sure was going to enjoy this for as long as it lasted. Tonight, though, was for her. For them.

He slipped her panties over her hips, exposing her to the heat of the fire. She was beautiful and swollen and glistening wet.

He wanted to feast on her. To use his mouth on her and tease her in all the ways he'd learned she liked.

He could suckle her where she was swollen. He could stroke her gently and feel her arch beneath his touch. He wanted to do everything and nothing all at once. He was content for a moment just to see her spread out before him, evidence of her pleasure glistening on her thighs.

He slipped the pad of his thumb along the seam of her body. A caress that was barely there. Her heat radiated against his skin. His thumb came away slick and warm.

"Tease." A choked whisper.

He licked his bottom lip, finally daring to meet her gaze. His eyes locked with hers as he slid his thumb into her heat, circling her where she was so, so swollen. She didn't look away as he stroked her softly. Her lips parted, though, and her breath came in quick, quiet gasps. She tensed as he continued to slide his fingers over her body. Gently, so gently. Driving them both wild with the simplest touch.

He leaned down, blowing against her skin where she was exposed to him. Felt her frustrated gasp. He smiled at her. Kept stroking her until she met his gaze again.

Then he took her in his mouth. Suckled her where she was swollen and sweet and...

Dear lord, she almost came right then. The pressure spiraled wide the moment his tongue connected with her, and he felt the tension wind up beneath his touch. He ached for this woman.

Her fingers were fists in his hair the moment she created the wave and started to come. She arched beneath his touch, offering herself completely, surrendering to the pleasure of his touch. It was beautiful, watching her body bow off the floor, to feel her shudder in her release.

The orgasm still shivered through her body as she urged him up until his erection was poised at the edge of her heat. "Now. I need you." She kissed him, hard and fierce. "I need you now."

He was there, just there, her silken wetness surrounding him. No barriers. No fear. Nothing but the tight, wet heat of her body surrounding him, urging him deeper. He gripped her hands, dragging them over her head as he slid inside her, inch by inch. Her body engulfed him, clenching around him tightly in that first touch of being home, really home.

He moved then, slowly finding the rhythm that pleasured them both. Moved when her fingers tightened in his. Drove them both closer to the edge until her body tensed and the wave cascaded over them both. Until her pleasure burst again, crashing over him, sending him spiraling out into the darkness beyond the storm.

And in the aftermath of it all, he held her close. Because there was nothing else he'd wanted more.

Chapter Eleven

They lay in silence, their bodies twined together in the glow from the fire. Quiet strokes. Soft whispers of breath on skin. She tried to hide the emotions burning behind her eyes, waiting to break free. To spill. They were there, just there.

She closed her eyes and waited, hoping, praying that she would be okay. That the crash would not destroy her.

The crash always came when you tried to ignore it. Sometimes it was within days, weeks, months.

Other times it took years. Decades away from the war before things finally burst out of the place where they'd been stuffed and ignored.

She lay cradled in his arms. She couldn't remember the last time she'd simply sat, comfortable and wrung out all at once.

Her heart was heavy and full, echoing every beat of his against her back.

She waited for the numbness to circle back up, to rise out of the darkness and drag away the echoes of sensation. To steal the pleasure at the warmth of his touch and leave her empty once more.

It didn't come.

Instead, sleep drifted over her and she stayed, feeling his arms around her, feeling safe and secure and *loved*.

God, how she loved this man. Loved him so much her heart ached with it. He shifted, nuzzling the top of her head with his cheek.

How could she have walked away from this? From everything that he meant to her? He was still here, still alive. Still warm and solid and steady.

"I remember the first time you deployed," she whispered, unsure if he was awake but needing to talk. Needing to release some of the pressure against her heart. "I was terrified you wouldn't come home."

She closed her eyes, seeing him again the day he'd walked out of the gym and toward that first deployment. She'd hated, *hated* being left behind.

She continued, needing to get the words out before she panicked and locked them down again. "I watched the news every day. First thing in the morning. Last thing at night. I was so afraid I was going to lose you." His fingers threaded with hers over her heart. Tightened just a little.

Letting her know he was there.

He was always there. He was the most steady thing in her life.

How could she have forgotten?

He shifted so her head leaned against his shoulder. "I wasn't prepared for you to go." He brushed her hair from her face. "I wanted to drag you out of that gym that day." He scoffed quietly. "I thought about converting to some religion that wouldn't let you out of the house."

She smiled in the firelight. "That probably wouldn't have gone over too well."

"I didn't say it was rational. Just that I'd considered it." His voice was deep against her back. "I don't know what I would have done if you hadn't come home, Sam," he whispered.

"It was a close thing." Her words choked off. Crushed in a wave of emotion that had been just there, just below the surface, waiting for its time to crash over her and drag her back into the emptiness of the abyss.

***

He felt the shudder escape her a moment before hot tears splashed onto his forearm. She'd been steadfast when they'd each deployed. Solid and stoic as first he'd shipped off to war, and then she'd followed. But this? This was different. This was a thousand years of emotion trapped and bottled up, finally breaking free.

Great shuddering sobs wracked her body. He shifted, pulling her closer, wishing he could lend her his strength. Wishing he could take away the pain tearing at her.

He held her while she cried. Whispered nonsense in her ear. And felt his own heart break as her sobs punished them both.

"It's going to be okay," he whispered.

She sat up then, pulling away from his warmth. "You don't know that." She swiped at her cheeks. She bit her lips together, trying to wrestle the emotion back into the vault. She placed her fist over her heart. "It hurts." A ragged, pain-filled admission. "And it feels like it's never going to stop."

He shifted, pulling her close until her head rested on his shoulder. Her tears were hot on his skin, leaving cool trails behind them as they traced down his bare chest.

"I want it to stop." She leaned back, wiping her eyes.

He cupped her cheeks, his heart breaking in his chest. "I can't tell you when it's not going to hurt anymore. I wish I could." He kissed her eyelids, her nose. Tasted the warm salt of her tears. "I wish there was some magical fucking pill that you could take to make everything feel normal again." Stroked his thumb over the dampness on her cheeks. "It's easier, when you don't feel. When you stuff it all down and pretend it's just another particularly shitty day at the office."

"I thought I could go to war and everything would be fine. I had some naive notion that the war wouldn't fucking hit home." Her voice broke. "That I would go and we'd sit on the FOB and drink coffee and do our jobs and come home at the end of the year." She wrapped her arms around her middle, holding her sides. "I was wrong. I was so fucking wrong." She finally looked up at him, and he saw staggering depths of despair looking back at him. He pulled her close until she sagged against him.

"I want out." He kissed the top of her head as her words sank in. "I want out of the Army." She leaned back to look at him. "I want to come home and be around my mom and my best friend's dad who was a better father to me than my own. I'm all they have left, and I can't take that away from either one of them." She swiped at her cheeks with the back of one hand. "And I won't ask you to give it up for me. I won't." She covered her hands with her face, the strength finally gone out of her.

"You never asked me." He cupped her cheeks. "You just ran, and assumed I'd be like everyone else in your life and let you go." Kissed her gently. "I love you, Samantha." He lowered his forehead to hers. "And if loving you means we leave the Army behind then so be it."

He held her then, cradled her in his arms as great wracking sobs tore through her.

Held her until his heart broke for her, until he couldn't tell where her tears ended and his began.

Until she was finally emptied out and still.

And even when the fire died down, he held her.

Because he was never going to let her go again.

***

Dawn came too early. It could have come at noon, and it would have been too early.

Her face was swollen. Her eyes gritty and heavy and full.

Last night's storm still swirled inside her. Less violent now but still there.

Still making her feel every ounce of ragged pain.

Patrick's arms tightened around her waist.

"It hurts."

"It always will." A gentle kiss against the back of her neck. "But I'm here. When the pain comes. When it gets too bad." His hand slid up, covering her heart. "I'm not going to leave you, Sam."

JESSICA SCOTT

"You can't promise me that." Denial that refused to be ignored.

"No one can. But that's not enough of a reason not to live. Not to love." His palm was warm and solid against her chest.

She closed her eyes. Took a deep, shuddering breath. Held it until her lungs burned. Released it quietly and opened her eyes once more to find him watching. Waiting. Always patient. Always calm.

"When we get back...I was thinking about making an appointment with Doc." Fear, naked and raw, in those tentative words.

He stilled. "I'll go with you. If you want."

She lowered her gaze. "I...I think I'd like that." She covered his hand with hers, threading her fingers with his, daring to meet his eyes once more. "I meant it. Last night when I said I wanted out. I'm dropping my REFRAD paperwork. I'm requesting release from active duty."

He was silent a long moment. "Looks like I'll have to study up on the Maine bar exam then."

She shifted, rolling until she could see his face. "I'm not—"

"You're going to be here. With my daughter." He brushed his lips against hers. "There's nothing the Army can give me to make giving up that time worthwhile." He lowered his forehead to hers. "I almost lost you from this last deployment. I'm not going to risk it again."

She nuzzled her nose against his. "You're going to freeze up here."

"Man, here I am offering you my undying devotion, and you're trying to get me to leave. You really know how to make a guy feel wanted."

She laughed against his lips, then turned, wrapping her arms around his neck and burying her face against his skin and simply holding on. He was steady and strong and solid and real.

The nightmare wasn't over. It was a long journey back from the darkness of the war. It would always be there, always lurking.

But last night, she'd taken a step. A single step that had started with a leap of faith. Of trusting this man who had been there for her from the very start.

She nuzzled his cheek, her heart full. For the first time in a long time, it wasn't filled with pain.

"Thank you for not giving up on me," she whispered.

And in that moment, she found something she'd feared she'd lost forever.

She found hope.

Chapter Twelve

Sam waited until the last presents were opened. Natalie was playing quietly by herself with her Lego *Millennium Falcon* she'd been eyeballing since last year and her mother and Thomas had gone out for a mid-morning walk through the snow. Patrick had disappeared upstairs a few minutes before.

Her hands shook as she found the gift she'd saved until last and followed Patrick upstairs to the room he'd shared with her since after the snowstorm.

She found him sitting on the bed, checking his e-mail. Embarrassed, he tried to stash his Blackberry. One look at her face, though, and the phone was forgotten, dropped on to the nightstand.

"What's wrong?"

She swallowed. And held out the manila folder.

He looked from her down to the folder and back again. "What's this?" There was caution in his voice.

"Gift card for more flannel." She tried to keep things light, needing a way to ease the tension around her heart.

His smile was warm, but the wariness didn't leave his eyes. "While I like what my wearing flannel does for your libido, we're going to have to discuss alternative clothing choices when we move." He looked down at the folder once more. "Sam?"

"Remember the day Natalie was born?"

Patrick went very still. Slowly, he reached for the folder.

She folded her arms over her chest, afraid he would see her hands shaking.

"When I filled out the paperwork for her parents, I left her dad's name blank."

He said nothing for a long moment. When he spoke, his voice was thick and filled with a thousand unsaid things. "That's why you never went after him for child support."

"There was no need. He wasn't her father. He's never been her father." She took a single step toward him. "She has a daddy. This…this just makes it official." She flipped the page. "It's the paperwork to amend her birth certificate. Apparently, you can just file a form from the Internet. There won't be an adoption. She'll be your daughter." She rested her hand over his heart. "On paper and in here."

She didn't expect to see his eyes fill. He ground his teeth, trying to keep the emotion in check. Her heart swelled in her chest but this time, the ache was something good. Something special.

A gift.

"This is the second best gift you've ever given me." He wrapped his arms around her waist, burying his face in her hair. A shudder ran through him. She tightened her arms around him.

"What's the first?"

"Letting me be there when she was born."

"What's wrong, Mommy?"

Sam took a step back to see their daughter standing in the doorway. Natalie looked between the two of them. "Are you sad?"

Sam looked at Patrick. He dropped to his knees in front of her. "No, baby, I'm not sad. Your Mommy just gave me the best Christmas present ever."

Natalie frowned. "But all you got her was a sweater and some coffee."

Sam covered her mouth and laughed. "Honey, I like my sweater. And that's my favorite coffee."

Natalie looked skeptical, the way only an eight-year-old could.

Patrick held open his arms until Natalie stepped into his embrace. Buried his face in their daughter's hair. Sam's heart ached. "Baby, Mommy just made sure our family would always be a family. And nothing will ever change that."

"But you two aren't married. Don't people have to be married to be a family?"

"No, baby, people don't have to be married to be a family." She looked at Patrick. "But I think I would like to be married to your Daddy very much."

"This is the best Christmas ever." A slow smile spread across her daughter's lips. She leaned forward with a happy sound, her arms around both their necks. "I got everything on my list."

Sam rested her cheek against Patrick's shoulder.

"Me, too," he whispered. "All I ever wanted was you. Both of you. Forever."

She closed her eyes and felt. Everything. All of it. The sadness and the happiness. The joy and the sorrow. It was so much. So overwhelming.

But at the center of it all was Patrick and their daughter.

Steady. Safe.

She'd almost lost him. She'd almost lost herself.

The war would never leave her.

But in that moment, she knew she had a chance to really come home. *They* had a chance. As a family.

Maybe they'd gotten their miracle after all.

More Books by Jessica Scott
Thank you for Reading!

Thank you so much to everyone who has ever bought one of my books, emailed me or just stopped by the blog, twitter or Facebook just to say hi.

Reviews help other readers decide whether or not to pick up a book. If you'd consider leaving one, I appreciate any and all reviews.

Want to know when my next book is available or special sales? Sign up for my newsletter at www.jessicascott.net

If you'd like to read my novels about soldiers coming home from war, please pick up my Coming Home series. It starts with *Because of You*. The series continues in *I'll Be Home for Christmas*, *Anything for You*, *Back to You*, *Until There Was You*, *All for You*, *It's Always Been You*. *All I Want For Christmas is You: A Coming Home Novella* will be available on November 11, 2014 and is featured in Home for Christmas: A Holiday Duet by JoAnn Ross & Jessica Scott.

If you'd like to read about my own experiences in Iraq and the transition home, please check out To Iraq & Back: On War & Writing and The Long Way Home: One Mom's Journey Home From War.

Keep reading for a special look at All For You

Prologue

Camp Taji, Iraq
2007

Sergeant First Class Reza Iaconelli had seen better days. He closed his eyes, wishing he was anywhere but curled up on the latrine floor in the middle of some dirty, shitty desert. The cold linoleum caressed his cheek, soothing the sensation of a billion spiders creeping over his skin. He had to get up, to get back to his platoon before someone came looking for him. Running patrols through the middle of Sadr City was so much better than being balled up on the bathroom floor, puking his guts out.

He'd sacrificed his dignity at the altar of the porcelain god two days ago when they'd arrived in northern Baghdad. It was going to be a rough deployment; that was for damn sure. Dear Lord, he'd give anything for a drink. Anything to stop the madness of detox. Why the fuck was he doing this to himself? Why did he pick up that godforsaken bottle every single time he made it home from this goddamned war?

The walls of the latrine echoed as someone pounded on the door. It felt like a mallet on the inside of a kettle drum inside his skull. "Sarn't Ike!"

Reza groaned and pushed up to his hands and knees. He couldn't let Foster see him like this. Couldn't let any of his guys see him like this. "You about ready? The patrol is gearing up to roll."

Holy hell. He dry heaved again, unable to breathe until the sensation of ripping his guts out through his throat passed. After a moment, he pushed himself upright and rinsed out his mouth. He'd definitely seen better days.

He wet his brown-black hair down and tucked the grey Army combat t-shirt into his uniform pants. Satisfied that no one would know he'd just been reduced to a quivering ball of misery a few moments before, he headed out to formation, a five- to seven-hour patrol through the shit hole known as Sadr City in his immediate future.

He was a goddamned sergeant first class and he had troops rolling into combat. They counted on him to do more than show up. They counted on him to lead them. Every single day.

Maybe by the time he reached thirty days in country, he'd stop heaving his guts up every morning. But sick or not, he was going out on patrol with his boys.

The best he could hope for was that he wouldn't puke in the tank.

Chapter One

Fort Hood, Texas
Spring 2009

"Where the hell is Wisniak?" Reza hooked his thumbs in his belt loops and glared at Foster.

Sergeant Dean Foster rolled his eyes and spat into the dirt, unfazed by Reza's glare. Foster had the lean, wiry body of a runner and the weathered lines of an infantryman carved into his face, though at twenty-five he was still a puppy. To Reza, he'd always be that skinny private who'd had his cherry popped on that first run up to Baghdad. "Sarn't Ike, I already told you. I tried calling him this morning but he's not answering. His phone is going straight to voicemail."

Reza sighed and rocked back on his heels, trying to rein in his temper. They'd managed to be home from the war for more than a year and somehow, soldiers like Wisniak were taking up the bulk of Reza's time. "Have you checked the R&R Center?"

"Nope. But I bet you're right." Foster pulled out his phone before Reza finished his sentence and started walking a short distance away to make the call.

"I know I am. He's been twitchy all week," he

mumbled, more to himself than to Foster. Reza glanced at his watch. The commander was going to have kittens if Reza didn't have his personnel report turned in soon, because herding cats was all noncommissioned officers were good for in the eyes of Captain James P Marshall the Third, resident pain in Reza's ass.

Foster turned away, holding up a finger as he started arguing with whoever just answered the phone. Reza swore quietly, then again when the company commander started walking toward him from the opposite end of the formation. Reza straightened and saluted.

It was mostly sincere.

"Sarn't Iaconelli, do you have accountability of your troops?"

"Sir, one hundred and thirty assigned, one hundred and twenty-four present. Three on appointment, one failure to report, and one at the R&R center. One in rehab."

"When is that shitbird Sloban going to get out of rehab?" Captain Marshall glanced down at his notepad.

"Sloban isn't a shitbird," Reza said quietly, daring Marshall to argue. "Sir."

Marshall looked like he wanted to slap Reza but as was normally the way with cowards and blowhards, he simply snapped his mouth shut. "Who's gone to the funny farm today?"

The Rest and Resiliency Center was supposed to be a place that helped combat veterans heal from the mental wounds of war. Instead, it had become the new generation's stress card, a place to go when their sergeant was making them work too hard. Guys like

Wisniak who had never deployed but who for some reason couldn't manage to wipe their own asses without someone holding their hands abused the system, taking up valuable resources from the warriors who needed it. But to say that out loud would mean agreeing with Captain Marshall. Reza would drop dead before that ever happened.

Luckily Captain Ben Teague approached, saving Reza the need to punch the commander in the face. The sergeant major would not be happy with him if that happened. Reza was already on thin ice as it was and there was no reason to give the sergeant major an extra excuse to dig into his fourth point of contact.

He was doing just fine. One day at a time, and all that.

Too bad guys like Marshall tested his willpower on a daily basis.

"So you don't have accountability of the entire company?" Marshall asked. Behind him Teague made a crude motion with his hand.

Reza rubbed his hand over his mouth, smothering a grin. "Sir, I know where everyone is. I'm heading to the R&R Center after formation to verify that Wisniak is there and see about getting a status update from the docs."

Marshall sighed heavily and the sound was laced with blame, as though Wisniak being at the R&R Center was Reza's personal failing. Behind him Teague mimed riding a horse and slapping it. Reza coughed into his hand as Marshall turned an alarming shade of puce. "I'm getting tired of someone always being unaccounted for, Sergeant."

"That makes two of us." Reza breathed deeply. "Sir."

"What are you planning on doing about it?"

He raised both eyebrows, his temper lashing at its frayed restraints. His mouth would be the death of him some day. That or his temper.

Right then, he didn't really care.

He started ticking off items on his fingers. "Well, sir, since you asked, first, I'm going to stop by the shoppette for coffee, then take a ride around post to break in my new truck. I'll probably stop out at Engineer Lake and smoke a cigar and consider whether or not to come back to work at all. Around noon, I'm going to swing into the R&R Center to make sure that Wisniak actually showed up and was seen. Then I'll spend the rest of the day hunting said sorry excuse for—"

"That's enough, sergeant," Marshall snapped and Teague mimed him behind his back. "I don't appreciate your insubordinate attitude. Accountability is the most important thing we do."

"I thought kicking in doors and killing bad guys was the most important thing we did?" Reza asked, doing his damnedest not to smirk. Damn but the man tried his patience and made him want to crack open a cold one and kick his boots up on his desk.

Except that he'd given up drinking. Again. And this time, it had to stick. At least, it had to if he wanted to take his boys downrange again.

The sergeant major had left him no wiggle room. No more drinking. Period.

"Sergeant—"

"Sir, I got it. I'll head to the R&R Center right after formation. I'll text you..." He glanced at Foster, who gave him a thumbs-up. Whatever the hell that was supposed to mean. Wisniak was at the R&R

Center, Reza supposed?

"You'll call. I don't know when texting became the army's preferred technique for communications between seniors and subordinates. I don't text."

Reza saluted sharply. It was effectively a fuck off but Marshall was either too stupid or too arrogant to grasp the difference. "Roger sir."

"Ben," Marshall mumbled.

"Jimmy." Which earned him a snarl from Marshall as he stalked off. Teague grinned. "He hates being called Jimmy."

"Which is why you've called him that every day since Infantry Officer Basic Course?"

"Of course," Teague said solemnly. "It is my sacred duty to screw with him whenever I can. He was potty trained at gunpoint."

"Considering he's a fifth generation army officer, probably," Reza mumbled. Foster walked back up, shaking his head and mumbling creative profanity beneath his breath. "They won't even tell you if Wisniak has checked in?"

"I practically gave the lady on the phone a hand job to get her to tell me anything and she pretty much told me to kiss her ass. Damn HIPAA laws. How is it protecting the patient's privacy when all I'm asking is if the jackass is there or not?"

Reza sighed. "I'll go find out if he's there. I need you to make sure the weapons training is good to go." Still swearing, Foster nodded and limped off. Too bad Foster wasn't a better ass kisser; he'd have already made staff sergeant.

But Marshall didn't like him and had denied his promotion for the last three months because Foster was nursing a bum leg. Granted, he'd jammed it up playing sports but the commander was being a total prick about it. It would have been better if Foster had been shot.

"Damn civilians," Reza mumbled, glancing at Teague. "I get that the docs are only supposed to talk to commanders but they make my life so damn difficult sometimes."

"They talk to you," Teague said, pushing his sunglasses up on his nose and shoving his hands into his pockets.

"That's because they're afraid of me. I look like every stereotype jihadi they can think of. All I have to do is say *drka drka Mohammed jihad* and I get whatever I want out of them."

"A Team America: World Police reference at six-fifteen a.m.? My day is complete." Teague laughed. "That's so fucking wrong. Just because you're brown?"

Reza shrugged. Growing up with a name like Reza Iaconelli had taught him how to fight. Young. With more than just the asshole kids on the street. He'd learned the hard way that little kids needed a whole lot more than attitude when standing up to a grown man.

"What can I say? No one knows what to think of the brown guy. Half the time, people think I'm Mexican." He started to walk off, still irritated by Marshall and the unrelenting douche baggery of the officer corps today. They cared more about stats than soldiers. It was total bullshit. The war wasn't even over yet and it was already all the way back to the garrison army bullshit that had gotten their asses handed to them from 2003 on.

"Where are you heading?" Teague asked.

125

"R&R. Need to check up on the resident crazy kid and make sure he's not going to off himself." He palmed his keys from his front pocket. Reza slammed the door of his truck and took a sip of his coffee, wishing it had a hell of a lot more in it than straight caffeine.

He ground his teeth. Things would have been different for Sloban if they'd gotten things right. If *he'd* gotten sober sooner. But no. He'd dropped the ball and Slo had paid the price.

He'd rather have his balls crushed with a pall peen hammer than deal with the R&R Center. He hated the psych docs. They were worse than the bleeding heart officers he seemed to find himself surrounded with these days. Just how he wanted to start off his seventy-fourth day sober: arguing with the shrinks.

Good times.

***

"I don't really think you understand the gravity of the situation, Captain."

Captain Emily Lindberg bristled at the use of her rank. The fact that a fellow captain used it to intimidate her only irritated her further.

Add in that he was standing in front of—no, he was leaning over—her desk trying to back up his words with a little threat of physical intimidation and Emily's temper snapped. Captain Jenkowski was built like a snake—tall and solid and mean—and he was clearly used to bullying his way through docs to get what he wanted.

Well not today.

She inhaled a calming breath through her nose and spoke softly, deliberately attempting to keep her composure. "I'm sorry, Captain, but I'm afraid you're the one who doesn't understand. Your soldier has experienced significant trauma since joining the military and his recurrent nightmares, excessive use of alcohol to self–medicate, and inability to effectively manage his stress are all indicators of serious psychological illness. He needs your compassion, not your wrath."

"Specialist Hendersen needs my size ten boot in his ass. He sat on the damned base last deployment and we only got mortared a few times. He's a candy pants wuss who has a serious case of *I do what I want-itis* and now he's come crying to you, expecting you to bail his sorry ass out of a drug charge." Emily could practically see smoke coming out of the big captain's ears.

Once upon a time she would have flinched away from his anger and done anything to placate him. It was abusive jerks like this who thought the army was all about their ability to accomplish their mission. The mouth breather in front of her didn't care about his soldiers.

It was up to folks like Emily to hold the line and keep the army from ruining yet another life. There had already been more than fifty suicides in the army this year and it was only April. "What Hendersen needs, Captain Jenkowski, is a break from you pressuring him to perform day in and day out. My duty-limiting profile is not going to change. He gets eight hours of sleep a night to give the Ambien a chance to work. And if you don't like it, file a complaint with my boss. He's the officer in charge of

127

the hospital."

"You fucking bitch," he said. His voice was low and threatening. "I'm trying to throw this little motherfucker out of the army for smoking spice and you're making sure that we're stuck babysitting his sorry ass. Way to take care of the real soldiers who have to waste their time on this little weasel instead of training."

The door slammed behind him with a bang and Emily sank into her chair. She had a full three minutes before her next patient and it wasn't even nine a.m.

A quick rap on her door pulled her out of her momentary shock. "You okay?"

She looked into the face of her first friend here at Fort Hood, Major Olivia Hale. "Yeah, sure. I just..."

"You get used to it after a while, you know," Olivia said, brushing her bangs out of her eyes.

"The rampant hostility or the incessant chest beating?" Emily tried to keep the frustration out of her voice and failed.

"Both?"

Emily smiled grimly. "Well that's helpful."

Moments like this made her seriously reconsider her life in the army. Of course, her parents would be more than happy for her to take the rank off her chest and return home to their Cape Cod family practice. The last thing she wanted to do was run home to a therapy session in waiting. Who wanted to work for parents who ran a business together but had gotten divorced fifteen years ago? At least here she was making a difference, instead of listening to spoiled rich kids complain about how hard their lives were or beg her for a prescription for Adderall so they could stay up for two days and prepare for their next exam.

Here she could make a difference. Do something that mattered.

Her family wouldn't understand.

Then again, they never had.

"Can I just say that I never imagined that I'd be going toe-to-toe with men who had egos the size of pro football linebackers? Where does the army find these guys?"

"Some of them aren't raging asshats," Olivia said. "There are a lot of commanders who actually care about their soldiers."

An Outlook reminder chimed, notifying her that she had two minutes. Emily frowned then clicked it off. "It must be something special about this office then that attracts all the ones who don't care."

She'd recently moved to Fort Hood because it was the place deemed most in need of psychiatric services. They had the unit with the highest active-duty suicide rate in the army. She was trying her damnedest to make a difference but the tidal wave of soldiers needing care was relentless.

Add in her administrative duties on mental health evaluations and sometimes, she didn't know which day of the week it was.

"Does it ever end?" she whispered, suddenly feeling overwhelmed at the stack of files on her desk. Each one represented a person. A soldier. A life under pressure.

Lives she did everything she could to save.

Olivia shrugged. "Not really." She glanced at her watch. "I've got a nine o'clock legal brief with the boss. You okay?"

She offered a weak smile. "Yeah. Have to be, right?"

Olivia didn't look convinced but didn't have time to dig in further. In the brief moment she had alone, Emily covered her face with her hands.

Every single day, Emily's faith in the system she'd wanted to help weakened. When officers like Jenkowski were threatening kids who just needed to take a break and pull themselves together to find some way of dealing with the trauma in their lives, it crushed part of her spirit. She'd never imagined that confrontation would be a daily part of her life as an army doc. She'd signed up to help people. She wasn't a commander, not a leader of soldiers. She was here to provide medical services. She'd barely stepped outside her office so all she knew was the inside of the clinic's walls.

She'd had no idea how much of a fight she'd have on a daily basis. Three months in and she was still shocked. Every single day brought something new.

She wasn't used to it. She doubted she would ever get used to it. It drained her.

But every day she got up and put on her boots to do it all over again.

She was here to make a difference.

A sharp knock on her door had her looking up. Her breath caught in her throat at the sight of the single most beautiful man she'd ever seen. His skin was deep bronze, his features carved perfection. There was a harshness around the edge of his wide full mouth that could have been from laughing too much or yelling too often. Maybe both.

And his shoulders filled the doorway. Dear Lord,

men actually came put together like this? She'd never met a man who embodied the fantasy man in uniform like this one. The real military man was just as likely to be a pimply-faced nineteen-year-old as he was to be this...this warrior god.

A god who looked ready for battle. It took Emily all of six-tenths of a second to realize that this man was not here for her phone number or to strip her naked and have his way with her. Well, he might want to have his way with her but she imagined it was in a strictly professional way. Not a hot and sweaty way, the thought of which made her insides clench and tighten.

She stood. This man looked like he was itching for a fight and darn it, if that's what he wanted, then Emily would give it to him.

It was just another day at the office, after all.

***

"Can I help you, Sergeant?"

Reza glanced at the little captain, who looked braced for battle. She was cute in a Reese Witherspoon kind of way, complete with dimples and except for her rich dark hair and silver blue eyes. If Reza hadn't been nursing one hell of a bad attitude and a serious case of the ass, he would've considered flirting with her.

Except that the sergeant major's warning of *don't fuck up* beat a cadence in his brain, so he wouldn't be flirting any time soon. Besides, something about the stubborn set of her jaw warned him that she wasn't someone to tangle with. She didn't look tough enough to crumble a cookie, and yet she'd squared off with him like she might just try to knock him down a peg or two. This ought to at least make the day interesting.

Reza straightened. She was the enemy for leaders like him, who were doing their damnedest to put bad troops out of the army. People like her ignored the warning signs from warriors like Sloban and let spineless cowards like Wisniak piss on her leg about how his mommy didn't love him enough.

This wasn't about Sloban. He couldn't help him now and that fact burned on a fundamental level. He released a deep breath. Then sucked in another one. "I need to know if Sergeant Chuck Wisniak signed in to the clinic."

"I'm sorry but unless you're the first sergeant or the commander, I can't tell you that."

Reza breathed hard through his nose. "I'm the first sergeant."

Her gaze flicked to the sergeant first class rank on his chest. He wasn't wearing the rank of the first sergeant, so his insignia was missing the rocker and the diamond that distinguished first sergeants from the soldiers that they led. Sergeants First Class were first sergeants all the time, though.

Her eyes narrowed. "Do you have orders?"

Reza's gaze dropped to the pen in her hand and the rhythmic way she flicked the cap on and off. He swallowed, pulling his gaze away from the distracting sound, and struggled to hold on to his patience.

"First sergeants are not commanders. We don't have assumption of command orders." He pinched the bridge of his nose and sighed. "Ma'am, I just need to know if he's here. Why is this such a big deal?"

"Because Sergeant Wisniak has told this clinic on

multiple occasions that his chain of command is targeting him, looking for an excuse to take his rank."

"Well, maybe if he was at work once in a while he wouldn't feel so persecuted."

The small captain lifted her chin. "Sergeant, do you have any idea what it feels like to be looked at like you're suspect every time you walk into a room?"

Something cold slithered across Reza's skin, sidling up to his heart and squeezing tightly. "Do you have any idea what it feels like to send soldiers back to combat knowing they lost training days chasing after a sissy-ass soldier who can't get to work on time?"

A shadow flickered across her pretty face but then it was gone, replaced by steel. "My job is to keep soldiers from killing themselves."

"And my job is to keep soldiers from dying in combat."

"They're not mutually exclusive."

Silence hung between them, battle lines drawn.

"I'm not leaving here without a status on Sarn't Wisniak," Reza said.

Captain Lindberg folded her arms over her chest. A flicker in her eyes, nothing more, then she spoke. "Sergeant Wisniak is in triage."

"I need to speak with him."

Lindberg shook her head. "No. I'm not letting anyone see him until he's stable. He's probably going to be admitted to the fifth floor. He's extremely high risk. And you're part of his problem, Sergeant."

Reza's temper snapped, breaking free before he could lash it back. "Don't put that on me, sweetheart. That trooper came in the army weak. I had nothing to do with his lack of a backbone." Reza turned to go before he lost his military bearing and started swearing. She'd already elevated his blood pressure to need-a-drink levels and it wasn't even nine a.m.

He could do this. He breathed deeply, running through creative profanity in his mind to keep the urge to drink at bay.

Her words stopped him at the door, slicing at his soul.

"How can you call yourself a leader? You're supposed to care about all your soldiers," she said, so softly he almost didn't hear her.

He turned slowly. Studied her, standing straight and stiff and pissed. "How can I call myself a leader? Honey, until you've bled in combat, don't talk to me about leadership. But go ahead. Keep protecting this shitbird and tie up all the counselors so that warriors who genuinely need help can't get it. He doesn't belong in the army." He swept his gaze down her body deliberately. Trying to provoke her. Her face flushed as he met her eyes coldly. "Neither do you."

***

Emily sucked in a sharp breath at Iaconelli's verbal slap. In one sentence, he'd struck her at the heart of her deepest fear.

It took everything she had to keep her hands from trembling.

Her boss Colonel Zavisca appeared in the doorway, saving her from embarrassing herself.

"Is there a problem, Sergeant?"

Sergeant Iaconelli turned and nearly collided with the full-bird colonel, who looked remarkably like an older version of Johnny Cash.

Sergeant Iaconelli straightened and his fists bunched at his sides. "You don't want me to answer that. Sir."

"I don't think I appreciate what you're insinuating."

"I don't really give a flying fuck what you think I'm insinuating. Maybe if your doctors did their jobs instead of actively trying to make my life more difficult, we wouldn't have this problem."

"What brigade are you in, Sergeant?" her boss demanded.

She watched the exchange, her breath locked in her throat. The big sergeant's hands clenched by his sides. "None of your damn business."

Colonel Zavisca might be a medical doctor but he was still a the senior officer in charge of the hospital. Emily had never seen an enlisted man so flagrantly flout regulations.

"You can leave now, Sergeant. Don't come back on this property without your commander."

The big sergeant swore and stalked off.

Emily wondered if he'd obey the order. She suspected she already knew the answer.

Her boss turned to her. "Are you okay?" he asked. Colonel Zavisca's voice was deep and calming, the perfect voice for a psych doctor. It was more than his voice, though. His entire demeanor was something soothing, a balm on ragged wounds. His quiet power and authority stood in such stark contrast to Sergeant Iaconelli.

Men like Sergeant Iaconelli were energy and motion and hard angles. And he was rude. Colonel Zavisca was more like some of the men at her father's country club except without the stench of sophisticated asshole. He was familiar.

"I'm fine, sir. Rough morning, that's all."

Emily stood for a long moment, Sergeant Iaconelli's words still ringing in her ears. He had no idea how much his comment hurt. She didn't know him from Adam but his words had found her weakness and stabbed it viciously.

In one single sentence, he'd shredded every hope she'd held onto since joining the army. She'd wanted to belong. To be part of something. To make a difference. He'd struck dead on without even knowing it. Her family had told her she'd never fit into the military. She fought the urge to sink into her chair and cover her face with her hands. She just needed a few minutes. She could do this.

The big sergeant didn't know her. His opinion did not matter. Her parents' opinions did not matter.

If she kept repeating this often enough, it would be true.

Her boss glanced at the clock on her wall. "It's too early for this."

She smiled thinly. "I know. Shaping up to be one heck of a Monday. Is triage already booked?"

He nodded. "Yes. I need you in there to help screen patients. We need to clear out the folks who can wait for appointments and identify those who are at risk right now of harming themselves or others."

"Roger, sir. I can do that. I need to e-mail two company commanders and I'll be right out there."

"Okay. Don't forget we have the staff sync at lunch."

Even this early, the day showed no sign of slowing down and all she wanted to do was go home and take a steaming hot bath. She'd been trying to work out a knot behind her left shoulder blade for days now and things just kept piling up. She needed a good soak and a massage. Not that she dared schedule one. She'd probably end up cancelling it anyway.

"There's that smile. Relax. You're going to die of a heart attack before you're thirty. The army is a marathon, not a sprint."

"Roger, sir." She waited until he closed the door before she covered her face in her hands once more. She could do this. She just needed to find her battle rhythm. She'd get into the swing of things. She wasn't about to quit just because things got a little rough.

Her cell phone vibrated on her desk. Oh, perfect. Her mother was calling. Not that she was about to answer that phone call. She couldn't deal with the passive-aggressive jabs her mother was so skilled at. Besides, she was probably just going to press Emily to give up on—as she put it—slumming in the army and come home.

She'd worked too hard to get where she was and she damn sure wasn't about to go limping home. How could she? Her parents had looked at her like she was an alien when she'd told them about Bentley. As though she had somehow been in the wrong for her fiancé's betrayal. As though, if she'd been woman enough, he never would have strayed.

If she ever went home again, and that was a really big if, she would do it on her own terms. She'd walked away from everything in her life that had been hollow and empty.

She was rebuilding, doing something that mattered for the first time in her life. Every day that she avoided calling home or being the person her father and his friends wanted her to be was a victory. No one in her family had supported her when she'd needed them. She might not have found her place yet in the army but just being here was a start. It was something new and she wasn't about to give up, no matter how much Monday threw at her.

Tuesday really needed to hurry up and get here though, because as Mondays went, this one was already shot all to hell.

About the Author

Jessica Scott is a career Army officer, mother of two daughters, three cats, and three dogs, wife to a career NCO, and wrangler of all things stuffed and fluffy. She is a terrible cook and even worse housekeeper, but she's a pretty good shot with her assigned weapon and someone liked some of the stuff she wrote. Somehow, her children are pretty well-adjusted and her husband still loves her, despite burned water and a messy house. No ZhuZhu Pets were harmed in the writing of this book.

Photo: Courtesy of Buzz Covington Photography

JESSICA SCOTT

CPSIA information can be obtained at www.ICGtesting.com
Printed in the USA
LVOW08s1627060916

503438LV00001B/161/P

9 781502 990198